Want

www.chellebliss.com

CHELLE BLISS

USA TODAY BESTSELLING AUTHOR

Published by Chelle Bliss © April 1, 2025
Edited by Silently Correcting Your Grammar
Proofread by Rose Holub & Shelley Charlton
Cover Design © Chelle Bliss
Formatting by Chelle Bliss

thank you for buying the print edition

Download the eBook version for FREE!

Scan the QR code below, add the eBook to your cart, and the 100% discount will be shown at checkout.

the eBook will be instantly delivered to your email via Bookfunnel

CHAPTER 1
BRAX

"HEY, handsome. What are you doing after this?" a regular at the bar asks. It's not the first time she's uttered the words either. If there were an award for consistency, she'd get the biggest one out there.

"Heading home to my girl," I lie to her because it's easier and will end the conversation quicker. She'll move on like she always does, finding someone else to scratch her itch.

"Darn it," she whines, barely able to find her lips with her beer bottle because she's so wasted.

"Want me to call you a cab?"

She shakes her head before slinking off the stool like she doesn't have many bones in her body. "No. I'll find a ride," she tells me with a devilish smile.

I have no doubt she'll find some man in this bar who will be more than happy to give her whatever type of ride she wants tonight. All I know is that man isn't going to be me.

"She yours?" Tate asks, lifting her chin toward the woman at the end of the bar.

"Mine?" I stare down at my older sister in confusion.

Tate rolls her eyes. "Your customer."

"Oh."

"Well?" she says when I don't answer her original question right away.

I gaze down the bar at the pretty woman who has a sadness about her. "She's mine," I tell Tate, figuring I could do one good deed tonight and see if I can make the woman smile at least once.

"Fine. You take that end of the bar, and I'll take the other. The place is a madhouse tonight. Freaking football play-offs. I hate this time of year," she grumbles as she starts to organize the liquor bottles under the bar.

"Whatever makes you happy." I give her a smile, hoping she'll stick around long enough to help me close tonight.

"No need to suck up. I'm staying until the place is empty."

I let out a laugh, hating how well my sister knows me. No one else knows me better than she does. We've been through some shit together, and it started at a very young age. She's mothered me at times, which I've hated the most. But she's always been there for me, and I've always been there for her. It's what siblings do—or, at least, what we do.

"Beer!" someone yells from the other end of the bar, Tate's end. She grunts loudly before stalking toward the impatient patron.

Chicago's in the play-offs for the first time since my uncle Vinnie played for the team. The city's electric with the possibility of making it to the national championship again after more than a decade. Thank goodness there are only a few more games before the entire season comes to an end and the bar goes back to the usual crowd, instead of filling every seat and then some.

I make my way to the other end of the bar, staring at the woman's profile. She's pretty, even with the blank look on her face as she stares up at the television screen. Her hair is long and flowing down her front, not giving much away when it comes to her body.

"Want another?" I ask her when her brown eyes finally meet mine.

Her smile barely touches the edge of her cheeks. "No. This is more than enough."

I give her a genuine smile back. "One isn't usually enough for our regular customers."

"I suppose not," she says in a soft voice. "I'm sorry I took this seat all night. I was waiting for someone who obviously isn't going to show. I'll tip you well since I took money out of your pocket."

"Darlin', the bar is full. You took nothing out of

my pocket. Nurse that beer for as long as you want. Whoever stood you up is an idiot."

"It's the story of my life. I swear I'm cursed," she mumbles as she lifts the bottle to her lips.

"It'll turn around. There're always a few jagoffs out there, but we're not all like that."

Her eyes search mine for a moment, and I wonder what she's thinking. She's probably running through all the clichés about bartenders. "I must be a magnet for them, then—or just purely unlucky."

"This seat taken?" a man asks her, coming out of nowhere.

"No," she says, not even looking in his direction. "It's all yours."

"Perfect," he replies as he slides onto the stool next to her. "I'll take a beer."

I don't know why his closeness to her bothers me, but it does. He's not a regular here at the bar, and he's alone. Which isn't entirely unusual, but he's acting a little too familiar toward her. He quickly spreads out, invading her personal space a little more than I'm comfortable with, and I'm sure she is too.

But it's not my place to say anything. At least until he does something that would require my intervention as one of the owners of this establishment. I grab a beer from the cooler and hand it to him before leaving them to watch the game and nurse their drinks in peace.

"Have you looked outside?" Tate asks me as I

make my way back to the middle of the bar after filling all the open orders.

"No. Why?"

"They weren't lying about the snow. It's coming down fast, and there're already six inches on the ground. I wouldn't be surprised if there's over a foot by the time we close."

"Good thing we can walk home," I tell her, hating the snow, but at least living nearby doesn't make it a problem besides the possibility of freezing to death.

"I hate this. I miss the sunshine and sandals."

"It'll be here before we know it."

She gives me a heated glare. "Liar."

"I can't think about the reality of how long it'll be cold. It makes it too tempting to move down to Florida like the rest of the family. They were smart, but our grandparents...nooooo. They had to stay in Chicago instead of moving to a warmer climate."

"It is their fault."

"Yep," I snap, mentally cursing my grandparents for our current predicament. We could be working at a bar on the beach, handing out drinks as the sun sets against the water and sand instead of the snow and cement.

I glance at the clock above the door. We have two hours until close. Thankfully, the game is in the fourth quarter, so the place should be clearing out soon.

Tomorrow's a workday for some people, but not me. I plan to spend the day sleeping in and catching up on shit I put off because procrastination is my superpower or maybe it's my kryptonite.

I glance down the bar and find the pretty lady leaning to her other side, moving her body away from the new guy who sat down. Immediately, alarm bells start sounding in my head. His face is turned toward her, but she's staring straight ahead, watching a game I figure she doesn't give two shits about.

He reaches an arm over to touch her, and she snatches her hand away, tucking it under the bar.

"Well, that's my cue," I mutter, knowing things are going to get dicey. Guys like him never seem to want to go quietly because they don't have a clue that their actions are unwanted, even if all the signs are there.

"Buddy, you need to move or go," I tell him before he even has a chance to look my direction. "Up to you which one."

"Why?" he says, finally turning his dark eyes in my direction. "I didn't do anything."

"Did she ask you to touch her?"

Her eyes dart to me and widen, the panic in them evident. "It's okay," she says, probably used to being harassed, but it's not okay with me.

"No, it's not. Moving or leaving?"

"You can't be serious," he chuckles deeply like I'm joking, but I'm as serious as a heart attack.

"I am. Pick one."

"I want to talk to the manager."

Of course he does. They always do. I don't know

why they think someone who's a manager would be okay with his type of behavior either.

"I'm the owner," I tell him, crossing my arms over my chest, trying to look as imposing as possible. I tower over him, but that doesn't keep me from doing whatever possible to stop him from acting out and playing the fool.

In my over ten years working at the Hook & Hustle, I've been in more bar fights than I can count on both hands. They've usually involved a guy who got a little too handsy with someone in the bar, and it's always our responsibility to step in. Sometimes they turn into an all-out brawl where the entire bar gets involved. Those are the worst because they are costly due to so many things getting broken.

I don't want that tonight. The last thing I want to do on my day off is clean up busted furniture and glass.

"Your place sucks," he says as he climbs to his feet and reaches into his back pocket.

"There's a bar down the street you may like better," I tell him, snatching the ten he throws on the bar as soon as it touches the varnished wood.

"Fucking ugly bitch anyway," he says before he stomps away and throws open the door to the bar.

Snow blows in, sending a chill through the room.

"You didn't have to do that," the woman says to me before she chews on her lip like she's trying to soothe her nerves.

"That isn't acceptable behavior in my bar—or anywhere, for that matter."

"It happens all the time."

"I have an older sister. I wouldn't let someone do that to her, and I won't let them do it to you."

Her face softens as she looks at me this time. "You're a good one."

"Sometimes," I tell her.

I try to be a good one, but I've had my share of shitty moments where I don't have the best judgment. I've never touched someone when they didn't want me to, but I didn't always treat women with the respect they deserved when I was a young dipshit learning how to deal with my hormones.

Tilly and Tate set me straight, though, and whatever lesson I didn't get through my thick skull, my father made sure I eventually got it.

"Well, thank you. The guy wasn't getting the hint."

"He probably never will."

"Do you think he'll come back?" she asks.

I draw my eyebrows together, surprised by her question. "Why would he?"

"He left upset, so maybe he'll be waiting for me when I leave."

Is this how all women think? Are they always looking over their shoulders, waiting for someone to get them? I can't imagine living like that. It has to be exhausting.

"I don't think so. If you wait around long enough, I can guarantee he won't be out there because he'll freeze to death."

"Then I'll take another," she says, pushing her nearly empty bottle toward me. "Better safe than sorry."

I smile as I grab a beer for her, hoping I eased some of the worry she had about the guy hanging around outside the bar. When I hand her the beer, I say, "Smart choice."

She beams at the two words like she hasn't received much praise in her life, which only makes me sadder for her than I already was.

I leave her be, figuring she's had enough from men today. First, being stood up, and second, having a man try to put his hands on her.

Luckily, the fourth quarter goes by in a flash since neither team had any penalties. Chicago won, which has the bar patrons in a good mood as they slowly peel out of the bar to head home to their warm beds.

But the woman from earlier has stayed put. Every time I glanced in her direction, she was looking over her shoulder like the man might appear out of thin air and do something to her.

"How often do you come across a creepy man?" I ask my sister as we're cleaning up some of the mess since things have slowed down.

"Like, what kind of creep?"

The answer doesn't sit right with me. "There are different types of creeps?"

"You have verbal creeps, touchy creeps, or the serial-killer-vibe creeps."

"Any of them," I tell her, shaking my head at the shit reality women face.

"Daily."

I freeze, looking over at her in shock. "Every day?"

"Well, that's usually what daily means, baby brother." She rolls her eyes at me like I'm an idiot, but I'm dumbstruck by her answer.

After a moment, I ask, "How do you deal with it?"

"Well," she sighs, loading a tray with partially filled glasses and dirty, damp napkins. "Murder is illegal, so I try to ignore it because I couldn't do hard time. I'm too pretty for that. If that fails, I usually have my pepper spray handy or have on a pair of steel-toed boots. A girl has to protect herself."

"That's ridiculous," I whisper, blinking rapidly as I gawk at her.

"It's reality, Brax. At least, it's my reality. It must be nice to be a man and walk through life without a single care in the world."

"I wouldn't say I don't have a care."

"Do you worry someone's going to snatch you?"

I stare at her without the ability to respond.

"Didn't think so."

"You worry someone's going to take you?"

"It happens. Maybe I've watched too many true crime documentaries, but if some big, beefy guy wants to take me, I don't have the build to fight him off. It's why my pepper spray is always ready and I took some self-defense classes."

"Jesus," I mutter. "That's so sad."

"Have you ever worried someone was going to sexually assault you?"

"Uh, no." I grimace as soon as the words are out of my mouth.

Never in my life has it even crossed my mind. Neither of the things she's mentioned have before. I guess I walk around clueless.

"Perfect example of male privilege," she says, lifting the tray and resting it against her hip.

"Hyperaware in dark parking lots?"

I shake my head.

"Listen to music on our walk home from work with those fancy earbud thingies?" she asks.

"Sometimes."

"Must be nice," she whispers.

"I'll start walking you home," I tell her.

"Wylder does every time I leave the shop or bar after dark. He refuses to let me do it alone, which is nice, but also pisses me off at the same time."

"I can understand that."

"That's life, though. As long as there are men around, we'll have to look over our shoulders. No one told me they were the real boogeymen. Not the fake ones under our beds as kids, but the strangers on the street who think they can do whatever they want when they want."

"I'm sorry," I tell her, suddenly hating that I'm a guy, even though I'm not a creep.

"Don't be," she says as she passes by and hip bumps me. "You're a good one, and I saw what you did for that woman. As long as the good ones are willing to stand up to the shitheads, there's hope for society and a possibility of change so it won't always be like this."

"Should I offer to walk her to her car?" I don't know why I ask Tate, but I do. I suddenly feel a sense of responsibility since my actions probably pissed the guy off more than she did when she pulled her hand away.

"That would be nice of you, but you don't have to. She's gone this long in her life without someone doing that for her. I'm sure she'll be fine. Anyway, there's too much snow for that idiot to still be outside. He'd be a snowman by now."

I dump a handful of empty beer bottles into the recycling next to the bar near my sister. "But would that be enough to not have you looking over your shoulder as you walked outside?"

"No," Tate answers quickly. "It'll always be in the back of her head, even in the middle of a blizzard."

"Then I'll walk her out when she's ready."

Tate touches my shoulder. "You're becoming

more thoughtful, Brax. I think you're finally turning into a man."

I give her the middle finger. "I've been one for a long time, sister."

"Debatable," she teases as she swats my middle finger down. "But old Brax wouldn't have thought twice about the woman after asking the man to leave."

Is it me becoming more thoughtful or aware of how the world works? Maybe it's the pretty girl with the pouty lips who looks like someone crushed all her hopes and dreams. No matter what, I'm not going to go through life with blinders on anymore, and I'm certainly not going to let the woman walk out of here alone.

"Hey," I say to her as she twists the beer bottle in her hands.

"Hey," she replies as she peers up at me.

"I'm going to walk you to your car."

"He's safe!" Tate yells from across the bar. "My brother's a good one."

The woman finally gives me a genuine smile. "I like her."

"She's a pain in the ass most times."

"That's sweet of you to offer, but I'm okay."

"I insist. I wouldn't be able to sleep tonight if I didn't."

She chews the corner of her lip for a moment before finally saying, "Okay."

CHAPTER 2
IRIS

THE CITY IS A MESS. I can't remember the last time it snowed this much in such a short time. The streets are covered with inches of snow, and there isn't a snowplow in sight as the bartender walks me to my car.

I feel awful that he's doing it when it's so cold outside, too. The wind is howling and bitter as it blows against my cheeks.

"I'm sorry," I say to him with my head down, trying to avoid the frigid air.

"There's nothing to be sorry for."

He's wearing a coat that's too thin, with his hands tucked into his pockets. No hat. No gloves. No protection from the weather. He has to be colder than me, but he isn't complaining.

"It's right around the corner," I tell him.

We walk in silence the last fifty feet to the private

parking lot where I parked my car to avoid a ticket for parking on the street in the snow.

When we make it to the entrance of the lot, I turn to him and say, "We're here. You can go back to the warmth of the bar."

"I'm not going anywhere until you're in your car, driving away."

His reply is so surprising, I almost trip over my own feet. Before I have a chance to face-plant in the snow, he grabs my arm and saves me from an even more embarrassing end to this already horrible evening.

"I got you," he says, and for the first time in a long time, I feel like someone cares more about me than themselves.

But the sad part is, he's a stranger.

What does that say about the men in my life?

Lucas was the biggest disappointment and heartbreak of my life. I lost all faith in the typical fairy-tale romance bullshit I was fed as a child. No man can say he loves a woman, only to leave her standing at the altar in her wedding gown with hundreds of people as witness to the most embarrassing moment of her life.

Of course people felt bad for me, but I heard the whispers about how there must be something wrong with me to have a man like Lucas ditch me in such a horrible way. I don't know how I became the problem when he was screwing someone else for months without my knowing. He never planned to go through with the wedding, but he was too chickenshit to cancel ahead of time.

"Thanks," I say as my cheeks flush from embarrassment more than the cold.

But to my surprise, he doesn't pull his hand away from my arm. "It's slippery out here."

I don't correct him. The last thing I want him to know is that I almost fell because of his niceness and not from the ice.

With my one free hand, I press the car remote in my pocket, making the horn beep. My eyes lock on the mountain of snow covering my small sedan. What a mess.

I can't believe I let Sandy and Mikayla bully me into this. They signed me up for a dating app without my knowledge, found a match, and scheduled this casual meeting for a drink. They said two years of swearing off men because of what Lucas did was long enough. It was time for me to get back out there and play the field. This was supposed to be my icebreaker, which is laughable because there's plenty of ice, but not because of a man.

When we get to my car, the bartender uses his arm to sweep the snow away from my door as I stand by with my mouth hanging open. The man is going out of his way to be nice to me, and I don't understand why. But I'm also not about to ask or reject his help, because the snow is ridiculous.

"Get in and get it started. I'll clean off the car," he says, still sweeping across the windows with his arm.

"I have a brush," I tell him as I open the door.

"That would help," he says with a smile.

He's handsome, but it's his kindness that's more striking to me than his good looks. Don't get me wrong. His features would make any woman with eyes look twice and possibly drool a little.

I reach into the back and grab the snow brush. "Here," I tell him, sticking it out to him as I situate myself in the front seat.

He takes it without a word and gets to work brushing off the huge pile of snow.

I push the start button, and nothing happens. I don't even wait another second before trying again, and there's still nothing but silence.

Don't do this to me.

This can't be happening. My car has always started. It's been the most reliable thing in my life.

"Start, damn it," I whisper to the steering wheel like I can magically will the damn machine with my mind. "You have to start." I take a deep breath before pressing the button again, but nothing.

The silence is deafening, other than the brushstrokes against the windshield. Now what am I going to do? The streets are a mess everywhere. I didn't see one cab on the walk over here. The snow is even too deep for them to run and make a profit. The train is nearby, but I don't live anywhere near a station. What a freaking mess.

"Everything okay?" he yells through the partially cleaned-off windshield.

"Um, not really."

He stalks back to my side of the car and pops his head into the cabin since I left the door open. "What's wrong?"

"The car won't start." I can feel tears starting to prick the corners of my eyes. They're quick to form in this type of frigid cold.

"Well, shit," he hisses.

My sentiments exactly.

"It's okay. I'll wait here for a tow. You can go back and get yourself warm."

A tow truck can easily get through this weather and drop me off at home before taking my car to an auto garage nearby.

The bartender blows out a long breath before looking around the almost-empty city. "I'm not leaving you out here alone. Come back to the bar and wait for them. There's no point in freezing to death because it could be a while before they make it out here. I'm sure they're swamped tonight."

My body's shivering on its own. Cold doesn't even begin to describe what I am right now. I imagine hypothermia wouldn't take long in the single digits. The last thing I want is to wait out here, alone and frozen.

"Are you sure?"

He holds out a hand to me, and I take it without a second thought. "I have a few hours of cleanup at the bar still before I can head out. Might as well have some company while I do it."

"I can help," I offer as I let him pull me up and out of my worthless sedan.

"I'll clean, you talk."

Great. Talking isn't my strong suit. Talking to a stranger is even worse for me. But in true Iris fashion, I say, "Okay."

A few minutes later, I'm climbing back onto the stool I occupied earlier. My fingers and toes are numb, and my face feels like it's on fire. Weather like this has me dreaming of living somewhere tropical someday. I wasn't built for these conditions, but was anyone really made to survive such harshness?

When the man has his coat off and he makes it back behind the bar, he stops in front of me and slides a cup of hot coffee to me. "This will help."

"Thanks," I say, giving him a genuine smile as I wrap my hands around the hot mug.

"I'm Brax, by the way."

"Iris."

He smiles back, the sight so stunning I'm momentarily breathless. "I like that name. It suits you."

"You look like a Brax." I don't even know what I'm saying at this point. I'm babbling from uncomfortableness. Not because of anything he's done. He's been great, but because he's too handsome and I would bet money on the fact that this man has had an illustrious past with women. He looks like the type where women have thrown themselves at him, begging for his attention.

"What's a Brax look like?" The smirk he gives me is devilish and somehow charming at the same time.

"Kind."

"Not handsome?"

The man does know he's handsome. I'm sure he's been told his entire life how beautiful he is. "A little bit." I chuckle. "I wouldn't say modesty is a word that is often used to describe a Brax."

"The man wouldn't know modesty if it smacked him in the face," a woman says as she walks out of the back room. "I would know because he's my little brother."

The woman is just as beautiful as he is handsome. The family must have some crazy genes. I wonder if anyone in their line has subpar looks. Probably not.

"I'm Tate," she says, giving me the same smile her brother has.

"Iris."

"I love that name. So soft, unlike my name."

"Your name is amazing. Unique."

"I like her, Brax."

"I do too," he says, which catches me completely off guard.

He likes me as much as anyone likes a stranger.

"I thought you were heading to her car?" Tate asks him as she starts to wipe down some of the round tables scattered around the main dining room.

"I did, but it wouldn't start. She's going to call a tow."

"I'm not surprised, with this cold. And good luck getting a tow in this mess."

"Great," I mutter against the rim of the hot coffee.

"Do you live far?" Brax asks me.

"I live up by Lincoln Park."

Brax whistles. "High-class and far as hell in this weather."

My shoulders slump forward on their own. "I know. I'm so screwed." I didn't mean to say that last bit out loud, but of course, my mouth just does whatever it wants sometimes.

"I have an empty apartment across the street. You can stay there for the night," Tate says, like what she is offering isn't a big deal.

Who says "I have an empty apartment"? In today's world, with the rising cost of real estate in the city, being able to own one place, let alone two, is a freaking miracle.

"You'd let me stay there?" I ask, turning on my stool to face her.

"Well, yeah. You can't sleep in a cold car, and the

bar is terribly uncomfortable. It's hard to find a surface that isn't sticky in at least one spot."

I wrinkle my nose at the thought of the stickiness. I can't imagine keeping a place like this clean with the volume of business they do and given that every drink they serve dries with a tacky film. "I promise to leave it in the same shape I find it. I can pay for the night too. You'd be doing me a big favor."

A big favor doesn't even quite describe what she's offering me. Without her, I'd be left without a place to stay for the night as a blizzard takes over the city. I am going to kill Sandy and Mikayla when I see them next.

My phone vibrates against the wood bar as if they knew I was thinking about them.

Sandy: How'd it go?

Mikayla: Yeah. I'm dying to hear the details.

I chew on my lip, letting my fingers hover over the screen as I debate how to answer their question without being too coarse.

Me: He never showed, and now I'm stranded with a broken car and inches of snow on the Southside.

Sandy: Fuccccccck.

Mikayla: Well, it could be worse.

Me: How? I could be stranded in the desert?

Mikayla: He could've shown up and been a murderer.

I roll my eyes as I read over her text.

Sandy: What are you going to do?

Mikayla: We're at Sandy's and can head your way to pick you up.

Sandy: We can be there in an hour.

Me: Have you looked outside?

Sandy: Shit. Make it two.

Me: Stay home. It's not safe out. I found a place to stay the night.

Sandy: Details.

Mikayla: What? Where?

Me: I'll tell you about it tomorrow. Night.

"Everything okay?" Brax asks as he moves around behind the bar, cleaning up from earlier.

"Just my friends checking on me. They're the reason I'm here."

"Were they supposed to come? They stood you up?" Tate asks.

"No. They set me up on a blind date, and he's the one who didn't show up."

"His loss," Brax says as his eyes flit to mine for the briefest of moments.

"Dumbass," Tate adds. "So many asshats in this world. Totally his loss, girl."

"It could've been worse, I guess."

"How?" Brax asks.

"I could be stranded with him."

"We're totally the better option," Tate says as she moves to the other side of the bar to grab a broom. "And it may be time to find new friends."

I giggle. "They're good people. They were trying

to do what they thought was best for me, even if I wasn't ready."

"Why aren't you ready? Bad break?" Tate asks.

My eyes meet Brax's, and for a moment, I'm embarrassed, but I don't feel like he'd judge me—or that she would either. "Something like that, but worse."

Tate gasps, stopping the sweeping motion and resting her weight against the broom. "Worse?"

I nod. "I was with someone for five years when he decided he didn't want to get married at the last minute."

"Oof. That's rough. Did he break it off the day before?" Tate asks.

"No. Not the day before. He decided it as we were standing on the altar together, about to say our vows."

"Damn," Tate mutters.

"Fucker," Brax growls.

"I would've killed him," Tate says, shaking her head. "My temper and embarrassment would need retribution and blood."

The smile on my face almost makes my cheeks hurt. It's been a long time since I've smiled this much. "I thought about it, but I wouldn't do well behind bars."

Tate chuckles. "Same, girl. Same."

"That man has no backbone," Brax says, giving me the look people usually do when they hear about what Lucas did.

Pity.

"And the smallest dick I've ever seen," I say, which is so unlike me but feels so good to get off my chest.

Brax bursts into a fit of laughter, folding forward to try to catch his breath. "Man, women are brutal."

"Sometimes the truth hurts," Tate says through a few giggles. "Sounds like he saved you from a life of misery…literally. Unless he was a pro at using it or other things."

"No, he was pretty awful at all the rest too," I admit with a little bit of embarrassment.

"Then thank your lucky stars you didn't settle for a life of pleasureless mediocrity," Tate says.

"You're right," I reply.

"Why would you marry him?" Brax asks, stopping in front of me and leaning on one arm, looking every bit the handsome man in my fantasies.

"Because I loved him."

"And now?"

"Now, I feel nothing."

"Not even hate?"

"Some anger, but it's been so long, he's not even worth the energy anymore. I rarely think of him at all, actually."

"That's healthy," Brax says. "Your friends are right. You're ready to move on."

"You think?" I ask, staring into his beautiful eyes.

"I talk to a lot of people. Being a bartender is kind

of like being a therapist. I see a lot of broken people, and you're not one of them, Iris."

"I agree with Brax and your friends. It's time to get back out there. Find someone who treats you well and makes you feel good about yourself."

Am I ready? Probably. Am I willing to trust again? That one isn't so easy.

"There're good guys out there still looking for love," Brax says.

"Are there?" I ask him.

"There are," Tate answers before he has a chance. "Brax is single and he's decent."

"Decent?" he asks her. "That's hurtful."

"Well, you're my brother. I've seen all the boneheaded things you've done in your life."

"He seems pretty great to me," I say without thinking.

Brax gives me a wink, and I almost melt into the plastic on the stool. "You're pretty great too, Iris."

Okay. Okay. Breathe, Iris. He's just being nice.

This man could have me falling to my knees, begging for his praise. There's something about him that has me acting unlike myself. I never talk to strangers about my past or problems, but they have me off-axis.

"Not to change the subject, but I'm just about done. You want the key to the apartment, Iris?" Tate asks me as she sets the broom back in the corner where she fetched it from earlier.

"If it's no bother."

"No bother at all. The shop is closed tomorrow, so take your time and sleep in." She fishes a set of keys out of her pocket and unclips a single key. "Just slide the key through the mail chute on the door when you lock up."

I take the key from her hand, wanting to throw my arms around her neck and pepper her with kisses as a thank-you, but I know it's too much. "I don't know how to repay you."

"Find yourself a great love like I found. That's what you can do to pay me back. No more shitheads."

"I'll do my best," I promise her as I slip the key into my pocket.

"I'll walk her over when I finish up," Brax tells his sister before bringing his gaze to me. "Unless you want to go over there now."

"I can wait. The warm coffee is too good."

Tate lets out a loud laugh. "The coffee is shit, but the company is good." She gives me a wink, and I know she's talking about her brother.

I have to agree with her. He's more than good, and spending time with him isn't a hardship.

The door to the bar opens, and a wall of a man walks in, shaking off the snow. My breath literally catches in my throat as my eyes travel across his frame. He has tattoos on his hands, which are exposed, a choice that's crazy in this cold.

"Ready, baby?" he asks, his eyes pinned to Tate as she grabs her coat.

"I could've walked myself home tonight, Wylder. It's too cold for you to be out."

"Fuck no. No way I'm letting my woman walk alone in the cold. Never going to happen.," he says as he slides his arms around her back, pulling her against him. "Let's get you home and in bed."

She smiles up at him, melting against his body. "You know the magic words. Bye, you two," she says without looking our direction.

"Bye, sis."

"Bye, Tate," I say, and I'm so damn happy for her. Not only is the man drop-dead gorgeous, but he loves her so much he'd walk through a snowstorm so she'd get home safe.

"Want a refill or something stronger?" Brax asks as soon as they leave.

"What do you have in mind?"

"A shot to celebrate moving on this year."

"You pour, I'll drink."

"I'll pour, we'll drink."

I smile, liking everything about how this night is turning out, even if my car is broken and I was stood up. The night could've ended so much worse.

Instead of ending on a bad note, I am going to share a shot with a hottie bartender and take a new outlook on life.

CHAPTER 3
BRAX

"THEY'RE SOMETHING, HUH," Iris says.

"Who?" I ask as I fill the shot glasses for a third time. Tomorrow, I am going to regret drinking so much, but it will be worth it, seeing Iris relaxed and with a smile on her face.

"Your sister and her man."

"They're nauseating at times, but it's also nice to see my sister so happy."

"That's sweet," she says as she lifts the shot glass to her lips. "Last toast because I'm not sure I'll be able to walk if I have another."

"You get a gold star from me. Three shots of this stuff would be more than enough for the average person."

Her gaze dips down to the filled glass. "Really? I barely feel anything."

"You will," I tell her with a chuckle, knowing the

punch of this stuff after it's had enough time to work through someone's system.

"Great," she mutters before doing this cute shrug with her shoulders and making a funny face. "Okay. Okay. The last toast... To finding happiness that makes other people nauseated."

I chuckle again, because she's using my word against me. "Cheers." I tap my glass against hers as gently as possible, so the contents don't slosh over the side and into her lap.

I watch her over the rim of the shot as she downs the liquor with ease. I take in her features, wondering how any guy could leave her at the altar. Besides ditching such a beautiful woman, you have to truly not like a person to embarrass them in such a public way in front of the people who care about them the most.

When she sets the shot glass back on the counter, she shivers. "That one wasn't as smooth as the others."

"I think we're done here." I snag the two empty shot glasses and the bottle of booze to put back for the customers on Tuesday. "I'll grab my coat and walk you over to the apartment."

"Why are you being so kind? I'm sure your wife isn't happy that you're coming home later than usual."

Her comment isn't lost on me. Is she fishing for information? Is she interested in me? Nah, she can't be. The woman hasn't had the best track record, and I'm sure hooking up with me is the last thing on her mind.

"No. No one's waiting for me. And I'm kind because that's just who I am and who I was raised to be."

It's partially true. I do have great parents as role models. That's the true part. But is that really me? Kind of. I could never leave a woman out there alone to face the elements and the city at night. It's not how I'm built. But if it were some random dude, would I care? A little, but by no means would I be walking them to a spare apartment above my sister's tattoo shop.

"You have good parents."

"I do," I tell her as we both pull on our coats, ready to do battle with the weather for the second time tonight. "The best."

"Mine are decent, but they've been overbearing ever since…" Her voice trails off, but I can guess the last part of the sentence.

"Rough," I mumble as I walk behind her while we head for the door.

"That doesn't even begin to describe them."

All conversation dies the moment we step outside and the cold and wind suck the air from our lungs. I don't understand how it's possible to breathe, but it is. I make quick work of the lock, and we hustle across the street like our asses are on fire and we're running from the flames.

As soon as we step inside Inked and I switch on the lights, she stops dead in the middle of the customer waiting area. "Wow. Wow. Wow. This place is amazing," Iris says as she gazes around the space.

It is impressive. I never thought my sister would make the place as beautiful as it is. Besides the family shop in Florida, most tattoo places I'd been in were dark and dingy, but Tate made it look more like an upscale spa. She wanted it to be welcoming for everybody, especially women.

"Wait until you see it in the daylight."

Iris drags her gaze away from the artwork on the wall to look at me. "I'm sure it's even more beautiful."

"It is," I tell her, and I want to say it's not as beautiful as she is, but I don't want to sound corny or for her to think it's the alcohol talking.

Iris covers her mouth as she yawns. It's late. Later than I planned on going to sleep tonight. I can't wait to crawl into bed and drift off.

"I'll show you up to the apartment, and then you can get some rest."

"Thanks," she says with a sweet smile.

Iris follows me to the back of the shop and the stairwell that's just as beautifully decorated as the rest of the place. The apartment is unlocked, which my sister often does when it's not in use. She refinished the space for visiting artists from out of town. The majority of the visitors have been our cousins from Florida who come back to Chicago to visit and do some tattooing while they're here.

I flip on the lights at the top of the stairs, illuminating the apartment.

"Wow. How is this place even better than downstairs?"

I laugh softly as I take off my boots. Tate would kill me if I left a trail of melted snow through the apartment. "My sister is a perfectionist."

"I can tell," Iris says, toeing off her boots on the rug near the doorway. "She could get big money for renting out this space."

It's bigger than my place. The entire top of the shop was converted into a decked-out apartment. My sister does nothing half-assed.

"The bedroom is over there, and the bathroom is next to it. I don't think there's anything in the fridge," I tell her as I stalk into the kitchen and open the fridge. "Just as I thought. Empty."

"It's okay. I can grab water from the tap, and I don't plan to eat anything until I leave in the morning."

"The bakery is open early."

"A bakery?" she asks, her eyebrows rising. "Where?"

"Next to the bar. My stepmom owns it, and it has the best cupcakes in town. The coffee isn't bad either if you like your coffee strong."

"You're speaking my love language," she says, her face turning pink before she clears her throat. "I love cupcakes, and coffee is my lifeline."

"Then you're in luck."

Iris hasn't moved. She's still standing near her boots, looking a little lost. "I don't know what I did to get so lucky, but thank you for all this, Brax. I don't know what I would've done if you weren't such a great guy."

"You would've figured something out," I tell her, but I don't know what the hell that would've been. Maybe she would've gotten a ride from someone in a few hours, but she would've had nowhere to wait while they drove across town on the snow-covered roads.

"I don't think so," she whispers, swaying a little, which I assume is from the alcohol finally making its home in her bloodstream.

"Are you going to be okay here?" I ask her. I know she's a grown woman, but this is a foreign apartment to her on a side of town I doubt she usually comes to.

"I think so." Her tone doesn't convince me.

I want to get home to my bed, but there's something inside me that has me pausing. "Do you want me to stay?"

She glances down at the hardwood floor. "No, you don't have to do that."

That doesn't mean she doesn't want me to. I've

spent my life reading between the lines when Tilly and Tate give responses.

"Would you feel more comfortable if I stayed with you tonight? I can sleep on the couch."

"I don't want to put you out."

Again, she's not saying she'll be fine.

"A big, comfy couch without walking home in a blizzard is not putting me out."

Iris twists her hands together like she's nervous. "Umm," she mumbles.

"I'll stay if you're comfortable. You're saving me from a very cold walk. I could freeze to death out there."

"That would be awful."

"Yeah." I smile at her.

"Please stay," she asks, finally telling me what she wants, even if I guilted her into it because she was worried about my well-being. "I don't want you to freeze to death."

"Thank you," I tell her.

"I appreciate you staying. Why don't you take the bed, and I'll take the couch?"

I shake my head. "That's not how it works, and if I'm honest, I've slept on this couch before. It's comfortable."

Iris raises an eyebrow. "You have?"

I nod. "A few times, but don't tell Tate."

Iris chuckles. "My lips are sealed."

Now, it's my turn to yawn. It's been a long day,

and I'm whipped from the ridiculous crowd we had at the bar for the game. "If you need anything, just shake me awake."

"I'd never," she says as she starts to move toward the bedroom where I pointed earlier. "Night, Brax."

"Good night, Iris. Sweet dreams."

She gives me a small smile over her shoulder before she disappears into the bedroom.

I stare down at the couch and wish I could strip down to nothing because I can't sleep well when I have clothes on. But if Iris wakes up and finds me naked...

I shake my head.

No, dummy.

The woman wouldn't be happy. She wouldn't wake me up in a way that could put a big smile on my face. It's stupid man-thinking led solely by my dick.

I strip off my shirt, scratching at my chest. I hate wintertime. The layers of clothes are suffocating. I can't wait until it's T-shirt season and I don't need to bundle up like I live in the Arctic.

I lie down, punching at the pillow I snagged from the closet a few times to get comfortable. When I close my eyes, I see Iris's smile and the kindness of her eyes.

My eyes pop open when I feel warmth against me. I peer to my side, finding Iris curling up against me. I don't say anything or even move.

What in the world? If you would've asked me to

bet on whether I'd find Iris next to me, I would've lost a lot of money.

I don't know what time it is or if any real number of hours have passed since I said good night to her and lay down.

"Iris?" I whisper.

"Shh," she says to me, snuggling into my side harder than before. "Sleepy."

I wrap an arm around her, leaning into whatever the hell is happening. I'm too tired and comfortable to get into it. And in all honesty, she feels good, and the warmth is an added bonus as the wind whirls outside.

When I open my eyes again, the smell of coffee hits me square in the face. The sun is shining through the windows like it's a warm, sunny day. I scrub at my eyes as I stretch my legs, hoping my back isn't wrecked from sleeping on the couch.

I throw my legs over the edge as I put myself upright, blinking away the sleep. My eyes immediately land on Iris, who's sitting in the kitchen at the island with her back to me.

"Iris," I whisper, my voice hoarse from sleep and the alcohol.

She spins around on the stool with a cupcake in her hand. "Good morning," she says sweetly.

"I see you found the bakery."

"It's the best place I've found in the city. It's a hidden gem." She reaches over, picking up a cup. "I brought you something. Tilly said it's how you like your coffee."

"Tilly was there?"

Iris nods. "She's so sweet. Tate had told her what happened, and I told Tilly you stayed the night to make sure I would be okay."

I lift my eyebrows. "Oh."

"She said she would've been upset if you'd left me here by myself."

That sounds like Tilly. While she's all for feminism, she's also for not leaving a woman in need. And other people may disagree, but Iris was in need of feeling safe in a foreign location.

"Did I do something wrong?" she asks.

I shake my head. "No." I push myself up, happy when my back doesn't tighten immediately. "My family shares everything, and Tilly would've given me an earful if I'd left you here."

It's her turn to say, "Oh."

"But that's not why I stayed. I wanted to stay here." I take the warm paper cup of coffee from her hand and sit down on the stool next to her. "Thanks for this."

"Did you sleep okay?"

I stare at her. "Do you remember last night?"

"No, silly. I was asleep. What happened?"

I blink a few times, wondering if she's screwing with me. "The couch," I whisper behind my coffee cup.

Iris's gaze moves to the couch. "Was it uncomfortable?"

I shake my head.

"Then what?"

I sip my coffee slowly, knowing Tilly makes it as hot as the surface of the sun. "You don't remember?"

She shakes her head, slowly pulling at the edge of the cupcake wrapper. "No, but now I'm not sure I want to know."

I chuckle softly. "You came into the living room."

Iris's big brown eyes grow giant. "I what?"

"You came into the living room."

She sets the cupcake down next to her coffee cup, and I can see the panic on her face. "And what?"

"You laid on the couch."

Her head drops forward, and she covers her face with her hands. "And what else?"

Do I tell her? We didn't do anything embarrassing. We both fell back to sleep. No touches were exchanged. No kisses given. "We slept."

"Together?" she gasps.

"We only slept. You crawled next to me and went to sleep."

"Oh my God," she says into her palms, shaking her head. "How embarrassing."

"Don't be embarrassed. It was nice to have the added warmth."

"Did I do anything else?"

"No, Iris. You basically told me to be quiet and that you were sleepy. I chalked it up to the alcohol."

"Damn it," she says as she finally lifts her head to look at me. "I must've been sleepwalking. I do it sometimes, and drinking usually makes it happen more often. It's why I rarely have hard liquor. This is so, so, so embarrassing."

"Nothing happened, Iris. Don't be embarrassed. I've done crazier things when I've had too much to drink. Snuggling up to someone doesn't even scratch the surface of bad alcohol behavior in my past."

She cracks a small smile, but it vanishes as quickly as it comes. "I hope I didn't make you uncomfortable. I'm mortified and so, so sorry."

I grab her hands gently, not wanting her to feel weird. "I was confused, but in all honesty, it was some of the best sleep I've ever had. Don't waste another moment thinking about it."

"I woke up in the bed," she admits, her lips turned down. "I had no idea."

"Well, I'm glad I was here, because who knows what would've happened if you would've sleepwalked without me to snuggle with. Have you ever wandered out of the house?"

"No," she says with a sigh. "That would be awful. It's been years since it's happened to me. Thank you for being so nice about this."

"If someone is a jerk because a beautiful woman

snuggles up to them, then it's time to run because they're an asshole."

Iris giggles as her face finally softens. "I don't know how I got so lucky to run into you, but I'm thankful for you making a very stressful twelve hours into something better."

"It was my pleasure." And it was. Being around Iris is easy, and whoever her ex was who left her at the altar is the biggest idiot on the planet. I hope he has perpetual limp dick for doing her so dirty.

"The tow will be here in an hour."

"The perfect amount of time to finish our coffee."

"Tilly sent you a pastry too." Iris reaches into a white paper bag and pulls out another of my favorites.

"You're making my day," I tell Iris as I take the chocolate-filled croissant from her hand. "Maybe the best morning ever."

"Why are you such a good guy?" she asks me.

I don't want to tell her that I'm usually not, but she makes me want to be better.

CHAPTER 4
IRIS

"WAIT. WAIT. WAIT," Sandy says, placing her coffee mug back on the table as she leans forward. "Let me get this straight. You were stranded in a snowstorm and stayed the night at his place and didn't do it?"

"It wasn't his place," I explain again. "It was an extra apartment his sister has above her tattoo shop, and no, we did not do it."

"Was he bad-looking?" Mikayla asks.

"No. He was probably the best-looking man I've ever seen. He's way out of my league and I'd bet he's broken a lot of hearts, and there was no way I'd add myself to that list."

"Having sex with someone doesn't mean you'd get a broken heart," Mikayla explains with an eye roll. "You can get laid and then never see him again. Lord knows you could use an orgasm."

"I have plenty of orgasms," I tell her, lifting my chin slightly.

"I'm not talking about masturbating, I."

"It gets the job done."

Mikayla folds over, placing her head on the table, and mutters something about me being a moron. "Ridiculous," she says a little more clearly before straightening and staring at me in disbelief. "You had the perfect chance."

"Did you get his number?" Sandy asks. "Please say you at least have that."

I shake my head.

Sandy and Mikayla groan in unison.

Sandy lifts a finger. "But you know where he works."

"Um," I mumble, already knowing where they're going to go with this. We've been friends since middle school, and I know them probably better than I know myself. "Yeah."

"You need to go back."

I widen my eyes. "No."

"Yes," Mikayla says with a devilish grin.

I let out a loud sigh. I wish I were the type of girl who would put her pride and heart on the line to go after someone I wanted, but my past has made sure any sliver of that person is gone forever. "I'm not going back. He didn't ask for my number either. If he were interested, he would've asked for it. I'm not going to embarrass myself by going back to the bar to see him. How mortifying."

"Babe, you need to go after the things you want," Mikayla tells me. She is never afraid to chase anything, including men.

"I didn't want the original date you set me up on. I'm just not ready yet."

"No one said you need to fall in love with him," Sandy says, like it's so simple not to catch feelings for someone.

"He was nice to talk to in a pinch and even better to look at, but I think it's best if he stays behind me."

"So, are you going to start dating casually again?" Mikayla asks.

The thought of dating makes my skin break out in hives and has me immediately scratching myself. "No. Not yet."

"How many years is it going to take?" Sandy asks as she stares at her phone. "Oh. Wait. I found another winner." She turns her phone screen toward me and then flips it toward Mikayla. "Look at this one."

"Damn. He's hot," Mikayla replies.

I have no response.

I didn't even focus my eyes on the screen before she moved it away. I don't want to look. I'm not interested in hooking up with men on dating apps. They aren't serious about love, relationships, or monogamy. No one can convince me that dating apps are anything except a tool to find people for sex.

"I swear your cooch is broken," Sandy teases me. "It's not like Lucas was even a good lay."

I blink a few times, hating the sound of his name coming out of her mouth. Not because her words are a lie, but I do my best not to think about him every day—or, at least, not more than once. "He wasn't the worst."

"Darling, I love you more than anyone," Sandy starts to say.

"Hey," Mikayla interrupts. "What about me?"

"You two bitches are my favorite people in the world. I'm not going to get into an argument about who I love more because it's a freaking tie."

"Whatever," Mikayla mutters and goes back to sipping her coffee.

"But to say he wasn't the worst isn't saying anything good. The man had a penis so small I'm surprised you could find it with a magnifying glass."

I regret telling them about his body. Maybe I knew we were never going to make it down the aisle and that's why I told them his biggest insecurity. I would've married him even without a decent-size dick. Sex isn't the most important thing in life…is it?

"You deserve to find someone who's going to make you walk funny the next day," Sandy says.

I stare at her for a minute. "That isn't real."

Sandy slaps her hands on the table and gasps. "Are you shitting me?"

Mikayla slides her hand on top of mine. "Baby,

it's very real and, also, very sad that you don't know it is. Things need to change in your life. Someday, you'll be old, and when you look back on this time, I don't want you to waste your youth and that hot body you've got grieving over some guy who wasn't worth it. It's time to use it before you lose it, mama."

"What's the name of the bar again?" Sandy asks.

"Hook & Hustle."

Her fingers are moving fast against her phone screen. "Found it," she says, and a sense of dread settles deep in my belly.

"What are you doing?" I ask her, trying to grab her phone, but she's too fast for me.

"Oh. My. God. Is this him?" she asks, turning the screen toward me.

I stare at the picture, seeing Brax standing behind the bar, looking every bit as handsome as he did last night. "Yeah, but don't you dare do anything."

"I think we need to have a drink there one night this week."

"No," I say quickly.

"Yes," Mikayla says.

Sandy's smile is so damn big I want to smack it off her cute face. "Just a beer or two. If nothing happens or he doesn't ask for your number, we'll drop it forever and forget he exists. But if he—"

"He won't," I interrupt. "Trust me."

"Oh. He will," Mikayla says, taking the phone

from Sandy. "Damn. That man is fine, and I bet his pecker isn't tiny either."

"You two are the worst." I shake my head, but they are right.

He didn't look like he had a tiny pecker, and if my memory serves me right from this morning, the tent in his pants when he was sleeping on the couch gave me proof.

I may have watched him a little too long as I sipped my coffee and ate cupcakes. I couldn't help it. It wasn't as if I would ever eat them in the bedroom, and it was on full display, begging for me to look.

"A few drinks and then he's in the past?" I ask them, making sure we are all on the same page.

Sandy gives me her best innocent look and blinks her big doe eyes rapidly. "I swear."

"Scout's honor," Mikayla says with two fingers in the air.

"When were you a Scout?" I ask.

"Never," she says with a chuckle. "But it sounded good, right?"

I scrub my hands up and down my face with a soft groan. "Can we not?" I ask them, glancing between the two of them.

"We must," Mikayla says.

Sandy motions toward Mikayla. "I agree with her."

"This may be the worst idea you two have ever had."

"Not if it gets you the hot guy," Sandy says, like it's going to be that easy.

If Brax were interested in me, he would've asked for my number, right? I mean, that would seem like the way the events would've happened. I don't have a ton of dating experience—definitely not as much as Mikayla or Sandy—but even with my limited knowledge, I think I would've known if he was interested, and he clearly was not.

"I'm not ready."

"Will you ever be?" Sandy asks point-blank.

I sigh again. "I don't know."

"You're annoying me," Mikayla adds.

"Hell, I annoy myself," I tell her.

They chuckle as Mikayla pats my hand again. "It's time to stop grieving what could've been and start getting excited about what will be."

"You're so wise," Sandy tells her with an approving smile.

Mikayla gives her a half bow. "I'm tapping my inner love goddess."

"You two are ridiculous," I mutter.

"You won't be thinking that when you're underneath that hottie, screaming out his name in pleasure."

I let my thoughts drift to what she described. Sex with Lucas was nothing like that. It was a quiet affair. Missionary was always his preferred position, and I didn't have a problem with that. Did he give me orgasms that had me screaming his name? Yes and no. He was successful in getting me to climax using his hands and mouth when I was able to concentrate fully. But they were never mind-blowing enough to have me screaming in pleasure.

I don't even know what Lucas would've done if I'd done that. The man was silent from start to finish. I barely knew when he was done. He'd just roll off and gasp for air.

Did he ask if I had an orgasm when he was done? No. Never.

But I never pushed him because I was happy the deed was over. Sex wasn't awful, but it wasn't something I looked forward to with him either.

"When should we go?" Sandy asks. "Tonight?"

"No. The city's still a mess from the storm," Mikayla answers.

"Not tonight. I was just with him this morning."

"Friday night, then. We're not putting this off any later," Sandy tells me.

"Fine," I grumble under my breath before straightening my back in the wooden chair. "Friday night it is, and then, he's in my past forever."

"What do you know about him?" Mikayla asks as she starts to tear apart her cheese Danish that looks like someone stepped on it because it's so flat.

"His stepmom owns the bakery next to the bar."

"Goodness. The man keeps getting better and better. I would kill to have someone in my family who owns a bakery." Mikayla takes a bite of the unfluffy pastry. "It has to be better than this garbage."

My gaze dips to the Danish. "It was the best bakery I've ever eaten at."

"He's getting bonus points," Sandy says. "And we need to go to the bakery too."

"It's not open at night."

"Damn," she whispers. "Another time, then."

"What else?" Mikayla asks.

"His sister owns the tattoo shop, Inked Southside or something like that, across the street. It was her spare apartment I slept in."

Mikayla shakes her head. "Can you imagine having a spare apartment?"

"Not on my salary," Sandy says.

"And she's a tattoo artist? This family sounds amazing."

"And he's a bartender?" Sandy asks.

"His family owns the bar," I explain.

"Do they own the entire damn block?" Mikayla asks, staring at me in disbelief.

I shrug. "I have no idea."

"If you don't marry him, I will," Sandy teases me.

"Maybe the sister is a total bitch," Mikayla tells her.

"No, she's nice. She was at the bar, and I met her. She's the one who offered the apartment to me."

I could see being friends with her. We didn't talk

much, but she was totally my type of person. She'd easily fit in with Sandy and Mikayla too.

"And her husband," I say and then whistle. "He was something else."

"How did you meet him?" Mikayla asks.

"He came to walk her home."

Sandy fans herself. "I would die for a man like that."

"He was covered in tattoos."

"You saw his entire body?" Sandy was quick to ask.

"No, but from what I could see on his hands and neck…I'm sure they were all over underneath his coat and clothes."

Mikayla sighs. "He's a dreamboat. Where do I order myself one of those?"

I shrug. "Hell if I know."

"Not online. I've looked. They're sold out," Sandy says with a giggle.

"So, he has a cool sister and a hot brother-in-law, his mom makes the best pastry in town, and his family owns a bar. Plus, let's not forget, he's hot and built. Sounds like the worst type of guy to date." Mikayla stares at me, and I stare back.

"I know. I know. He sounds like the total package, but he's still single, and at our age, that means something is wrong."

Mikayla smacks my hand this time. "Bitch, we're all single. There's nothing wrong with us."

"Lala, you are kind of a nympho," Sandy tells her, lifting her hands. "That's a hard sell when it comes to being wife material."

"What man wouldn't want a woman who wants to have sex every single day?" she asks Sandy.

"Clearly, they're not trampling each other to make it happen," Sandy replies.

"What about you?" Mikayla says back to Sandy. "You're a clean freak and scare off every man who isn't as tidy as you."

"I like things how I like things." Sandy shrugs. "I won't live in filth just to have a ring on my finger. I'm picky."

Mikayla rolls her eyes. "You wash your sheets every day."

Sandy tilts her head, giving Mikayla a pointed stare. "And?"

"It's not normal," Mikayla replies.

"It's my normal." Sandy gives Mikayla the middle finger before grabbing her coffee, trying not to get into her obsessive need to clean. "I'm not forcing you to wash your sheets every day."

"If mine make it into the washing machine once every two weeks, it's a miracle," Mikayla tells her.

Sandy wrinkles her nose. "That's gross."

"You two are something else," I say.

"How often do you wash your sheets?" Sandy asks, wanting my vindication.

"Every weekend."

"That's normal," Mikayla says, "and impressive."

"Maybe Mr. Romeo doesn't wash his sheets ever, and that's why he hasn't found a wife," Sandy explains. "Any sane woman would run the other way after getting one whiff."

"His name is Brax," I correct her.

"Brax doesn't look smelly," she says as she enlarges his picture standing behind the bar, because she never scrolled away from it. "Does he?" That question is pointed at Mikayla.

Mikayla leans over, glancing down at the photo. "No. He looks like he'd wake up smelling like pine and man."

I roll my eyes. "What is wrong with you?"

"Too many things to get into right now." Mikayla winks at me. "But there are some guys who look smelly and are smelly. You know what I mean?"

"No." My friends are so damn quirky, and I love them for it most times, but this isn't one of them.

"Totally like pine and man. Maybe with a hint of bourbon too," Sandy adds, ignoring me.

"I'm going to smell him on Friday," Mikayla says. "But I'll be quick so he doesn't notice I'm doing it."

"Jesus," I mutter, resting my forehead in my hand, wishing I could take back agreeing to go back to the bar to see him. "You two are crazier than I ever realized."

"You have no idea," Sandy says, giving me a cute little wink when I lift my head and look in her direction. "But you will."

CHAPTER 5
BRAX

FAMILY DINNERS HAVE BECOME MORE chaotic, or maybe I've finally grown up enough to notice.

Feeding a small army, half of whom think they're in charge of the preparation, is exhausting. If we didn't own a bar and restaurant, I don't know how we'd ever be able to prepare so much food in such a short amount of time.

I've already been chased out of the kitchen by Aunt Daphne, and surprisingly, I'm okay with it. When I go to grab a beer, Tate's sitting at the bar with Ma.

"So…" Tate says, drawing out the word. "How did last night go?"

I glance up at her, knowing she's talking to me and not our stepmom. "Fine."

"You stayed with her?" she asks.

"Didn't feel right leaving her alone in a place she wasn't familiar with on a side of town she doesn't know." I take a sip of the beer, wishing it were a warm night outside instead of the frozen tundra that's currently blanketing the city.

"She was lovely," Ma says as she touches the rim of her martini glass. She's always been a sucker for sweet drinks, and tonight's no exception. I made her favorite, a chocolate martini with top-shelf liquor.

"Wait." Tate turns her head to stare at Tilly. "You met her?"

Ma smiles at Tate and nods. "She walked over to get some breakfast this morning, along with two coffees."

"You didn't tell me you met her," Tate says to her.

"Sorry, kiddo. I didn't think it was important."

Tate drags her gaze back to me. "Did you sleep with her?"

I shake my head and somehow don't choke on my beer as I swallow. "I don't sleep with every woman I meet, Tate."

Tate snorts. "Since when?"

"I told you. I'm getting serious about my future, and that doesn't include sleeping with the entire city."

"You've blown through most of them anyway," Tate replies with a chuckle. "And you can get serious and still have some fun."

I glance over at Ma, but she's busy staring down into her drink like she's searching for something. She doesn't want to hear this conversation as much as I don't want her to. "I'm turning over a new leaf. I was a complete gentleman."

"When are you seeing her again?" Tate asks.

"Never."

Tate gawks at me, blinking a few times. "What? Why?"

"I didn't get her number."

Tate hangs her head, muttering how I'm an idiot under her breath. "Why wouldn't you get her number? You get everyone's number."

"I don't know, Tate." I blow out a breath and lean over the bar, taking up some of the space between Tate and Ma.

"That's a shame," Ma says, using the tiny red straw to stir her martini. "I really liked her."

"She knows where to find me. If she's interested, she'll be back."

"You really are an idiot," Tate says as she lifts her beer to her lips, glaring at me over her hand.

"My baby isn't an idiot," Gram says, coming up next to me and snaking her arm around my waist. "He's a fine man."

"Gram," Tate says as she shakes her head. "Your fine man has a reputation with the ladies."

"So did your grandpa when I met him." Gram gives Tate a big smile.

But my sister doesn't smile back. She jerks her

head back and makes a gagging noise. "Ick, Gram. I don't want to hear that about Grandpa."

"Well, sweetie, we were all young once. No one is an angel, and your grandpa certainly wasn't. Don't even get me started on his time in prison."

Tate's eyes go wide. "What? I thought that was my childhood imagination playing tricks on me. I remember something about him going away when I was little, but I thought my memory had to be wrong."

Gram laughs. "I wish it were, but that doesn't mean it's not funny, even after all these years."

"What in the world," Tate says as she stares at our grandma in disbelief.

"But he's not that man anymore," Gram says, as if that somehow makes up for all the insanity he put her through in their marriage. "Enough about the past. What are we talking about?"

"Brax had a sleepover with a woman, and all they did was sleep," Ma says, entering the conversation a little more.

Gram peers up at me with a concerned look. "Are you sick, baby?"

I lean over and kiss her cheek. "I'm fine. Just trying to be better."

"Is she the one?" Gram asks as she tightens her arm around my middle.

"Oh hell, Gram. I don't know. Do people really know that after meeting once?"

"I heard they do. I didn't feel that way. I couldn't stand your grandpa, but eventually, he wore me down, and the rest is history."

"Wow," Tate mutters as she leans back in the chair, looking bewildered. "That's so romantic. Everything every little girl hopes for in a courtship."

"You've watched too many movies, baby. Not every relationship starts with a sprinkle of magic."

"This conversation is depressing," Tate adds.

"When are you seeing her again?" Gram asks.

"I don't think I am. I didn't get her number. I only know her name."

"Dumb boy," Gram whispers.

"Exactly," Tate agrees.

"What's everyone talking about?" Dad asks as he walks up and takes the seat next to Ma.

"Your son being a dumbass," Tate tells him.

Dad blows out a loud breath as he scrubs his hand down his face. "Well, okay."

"He didn't get a woman's number," Ma explains, motioning toward me with her hand.

"Are you feeling okay?" Dad asks.

"Exactly what I asked," Gram replies.

I raise my hands as I straighten. "I'm fine. Sheesh. A man can spend a little time with a woman and not ask for her number. It's not a crime."

"Yeah, but we're talking about you," Tate says.

"Are you sick?" Wylder asks as he sits down at the

other end of the group next to my sister. "What's wrong?"

"I'm not sick," I say with a growl. "You people overreact about everything."

Wylder leans over to Tate and whispers, "What did I miss?"

"My brother is an idiot," is her reply.

"Most men are," Wylder replies.

"Speak for yourself," I tell him with a chin lift.

My family, as much as I love them, is so freaking nosy and opinionated about everything. Working together doesn't make anything easier. Nothing is private, but it never has been. I should be used to it by now.

"If she likes me, she'll be back. I left the ball in her court."

"Does she know you're interested?" Dad asks.

I shrug. "I don't know. Clearly, I don't know much about women."

"Obviously," Tate mumbles before I can finish the statement.

"I never knew asking someone for their number was that important. She could've asked for mine, you know."

"Yeah, that doesn't happen," Tate says.

"Women have asked for my number, sister."

"Not the kind you want to marry," she replies.

I snap my lips shut at her response. I hate to say it, but she's right. All of the women who have asked for my number in the past aren't the type I'd ever consider getting into any sort of long-term relationship with, let alone marry. It was all about fucking, plain and simple.

"Is this the sweet woman you were talking about this morning?" Dad asks Ma, trying to catch up to the conversation.

"Yeah," she says as she places her hand over his.

They're my inspiration. My entire life, I've watched them be completely devoted to each other. Well, not my entire life. My birth mom passed away when I was little, and my dad met Tilly a few years later. I barely remember a time without Tilly in my life. She's really the only mom I have memories of, which makes me sad, but I'm extremely happy I have her to fill the void.

"How did she pay?" Dad asks Ma.

Ma stares at him and doesn't reply.

"Did she use a credit card?" he asks her.

Ma nods. "Yeah."

"So, you know her full name."

I stare at him as I push my eyebrows together. "Don't even say it," I tell him.

"You can find her online, then. Maybe reach out and say hello," he explains, like it's really that easy.

"That's super creepy, Dad," Tate tells him, coming to my rescue from Dad's grand plan.

"Is it?" He scratches at the scruff on his jawline. "I don't think so."

"It's kind of romantic," Ma says, giving him a sweet smile. She thinks every idea the man has is romantic.

"If you're a stalker," Tate adds.

"Creepy is better than nothing," Gram says from where she's still stuck to me like glue.

I glance around the bar, looking for a rescue from this batshit crazy conversation. I lock eyes with Vinnie. He'll save me.

But before I have a chance to excuse myself, he heads our way. "What's up?" he asks when he's close enough to hear our response over all the talking.

"I'm an idiot," I tell him, saving time.

Vinnie chuckles. "Well, at least we're in agreement."

I give my uncle the middle finger, and he lifts his hands. "You said it, buddy. Not me."

"My dad wants me to look up some woman on the internet and send her a message."

Vinnie's face scrunches up exactly how I'd expect it to. "He wants you to stalk her?"

"See?" I say, waving a hand in my uncle's direction. "Stalker."

Dad shrugs. "Fine. Maybe by some miracle, she'll show back up here at the bar."

"If she comes back to the bakery, do you want me to ask for her number?"

Mortification overwhelms me. "No, Ma. That's not any better."

Tate giggles. "I would love to watch that conversation unfold. You'd totally lose your man card if Ma asks a girl out for you."

"I think it's sweet," Gram adds.

"Ma, I think Daphne needs help in the back," Vinnie tells her.

"Oh," she says before peeling away from me and disappearing.

"Why'd you do that?" Tate asks our uncle.

"Because Daphne literally texted in the group chat that she needed Ma," he says, showing Tate his phone screen.

"I thought you were just trying to get rid of her," Tate tells him as he places his phone in his back pocket.

"Nah. Ma's cool. She put up with all my insanity. She can handle a conversation about romance, although her idea of relationships and acceptable behavior may be a bit wonky."

"A bit?" Dad says to his brother and snorts. "It's a lot wonky."

"Dad was such a dick back in the day," Vinnie replies.

"That's my grandpa," Tate says, lifting her chin at their negative conversation.

"He is that, but he was still a dick," Dad says. "Thank goodness he's not that man anymore."

"Can we get back to talking about Brax and not Grandpa?" Tate says.

"Food's ready," Gram says as she walks out into the bar from the kitchen.

I've never been so happy to eat. As long as everyone is jamming food into their mouths, they won't be able to talk about me.

Like we do every week, everyone files into the kitchen to grab the food, along with the plates, silverware, and everything else we need.

After I dish out a small amount of food, I find a table near the window and hope no one will sit next to me. I am already talked out.

"What's shakin', bacon?" Lucio asks as he sits down next to me, killing any hope of a quiet meal.

"Not much, Unc. You?"

"Eh. Same shit, different day." He stabs at his pasta like he's starving to death and hasn't had a decent meal in days. "Wish it were summer."

"Same," I say with a mouthful of rigatoni.

"Dating anyone?"

I peer up at him in surprise. He doesn't usually talk about relationships. He and Aunt Delilah have been married for twenty years, and just like my parents, they're crazy about each other.

"No. Single as the day I was born."

"Shame," he mutters as he moves the food around on his plate like he's searching for the right bite. "Are you taking a break?"

"No, Unc, but I'm not scouring the dating apps to find someone either."

"It'll happen when you least expect," he says.

And I wonder if it already has. I shake my head, knowing I'm being an idiot. My dream girl didn't walk into the bar last night and then I let her leave without getting at least her basic contact information. All I know is her face, her name, and how she feels curled against my side.

"Delilah wandered into the bar with Lulu in her arms. I never thought I'd be sitting here with her decades later. Life is funny like that somehow."

"Can I sit here?" Lulu asks, holding two plates. One is loaded with salad, and the other has nothing except dessert.

"Yeah, sweetheart. Sit. Sit."

I stare at her plate in confusion. "What's that?" I point to her plates with my fork.

"I'm saving the main-course calories for my dessert." She doesn't even look at me when she answers. She's too focused on the chocolate cake and cupcakes she grabbed from the far end of the bar. "These hips didn't make themselves."

"That's not healthy, baby girl," Lucio, her dad for all intents and purposes, says to her.

"Salad's very healthy," she tells him before she shoves a big forkful of vegetables into her mouth.

Lucio shakes his head but lets the conversation drop.

"What are you looking at?" she asks me.

"Nothing," I tell her. I mean, I was looking at her

food, but I wasn't thinking anything except I hope there's some cake left by the time I'm done eating. "Just that you were smart to grab the cake before everyone else."

"Thanks, cuz. I'm not a dummy, but from what I hear, you are," she says with a smile as her eyes flit toward my sister.

"What happened?" Lucio asks her.

"Nothing, Unc." I glare at my cousin, wanting to let the conversation die off as quickly as her dessert in place of a meal did. "How's college?"

Lulu groans. "Last semester and it's killing me."

"But think, you'll be done soon, and then you'll be making bank."

She snorts and shakes her head. "Hopefully the business degree will be worth it."

"I'm sure you've learned tons of useful stuff," I tell her. "You're going to be your own boss."

"Your lips to God's ears," she mumbles. "Too bad the startup didn't pan out, but I have a few other ideas I'm working out in my head to start my own business."

"There's always a spot for you here," I say, earning a smile from her.

"I'm so proud of you," Uncle Lucio says to Lulu. "You've worked so hard for this."

And she has. Lulu was never the best student. Math wasn't an easy subject for her, and she spent hours every week going to tutoring so she could pass her math requirements in high school and then did it again for college.

"Thanks, Dad. I'm just ready to get out there and start my own business."

Lulu isn't much younger than me, but she took some time off after high school to backpack around Europe. She said she wanted to see the world because she hadn't been out of Chicago much in her life. She came back an entirely different person, one who seemed more content with who she was and where she was headed in life.

"You'll figure it out, cousin. Don't worry," I tell her. "We have enough connections in the area, anything you do will be successful."

"I want to accomplish things because of my ability and merits. Not because I knew someone's uncle."

"There's no shame in how you get a job, as long as you get it," Uncle Lucio tells his daughter. "We could all use a hand sometimes."

"Brax knows all about that," Mason, my little brother, says as he sits down with us. "Don't ask me how I know, but I do."

"You're an asshole," I say, kicking his chair with enough force to make his body jolt.

"Dad told me he wants you to stalk someone."

Lucio starts to choke on his pasta. "What?" he asks in a strangled voice, barely able to breathe past the noodle in his throat.

"You okay?" Lulu asks her dad.

"Fine, sweetheart," he says and clears his throat. "What is your dad telling you to do?"

I explain the entire situation. No point in hiding it. The entire family will know about it before we leave the bar tonight. Again, there's no such thing as privacy with this group.

"Yeah, don't do that," Lulu says. "That would creep me the hell out."

I nod. "I told him."

"We've been out of the dating world too long. Your dad doesn't understand the boundaries when it comes to social media and what's acceptable behavior."

"Thank you," I tell my uncle.

"But you could maybe look her up and send her some flowers."

Lulu drops her forkful of cake on her plate. "Dad, that's no better. Sheesh. What's wrong with your generation?"

Lucio shakes his head. "Honey, we're romantic."

"That's not romantic. That's pathological," she replies as she grabs her fork again.

"How hot are we talking?" Mason asks me. "Like melt the snow outside hot or what?"

I stare at my brother, trying to remember if we dropped him on his head when he was little. "She was beautiful."

"You're a dummy," he replies.

"See." Lulu smirks. "We're all in agreement."

"Eat your cake," I tell her, motioning toward her plate with my fork.

"If it was meant to be, you'll find your way back to her, kid," Uncle Lucio says. "The universe won't be able to keep you apart."

I stare at him without a response.

Is he right?

Is there such a thing as fate?

I've never believed in it. But for the first time ever, I hope he's right.

CHAPTER 6
IRIS

IT'S FRIDAY. The day I promised my two best friends we'd go back to the bar to see if he remembers me. It's a long shot. I'm sure he meets more than a handful of beautiful women every week.

It's not that I'm not memorable. I'm pretty enough to catch most men's eyes even when I'm not trying. But if he had been interested, he would've said something to me or asked for my phone number at the very least…right?

"I feel stupid." I stare at my reflection in the glass outside the bar. "I can't believe I let you two talk me into this. You have the worst ideas."

Sandy bumps me with her shoulder as her eyes catch my reflection. "You won't be saying that when his dick—"

"Stop," I say quickly, turning to face her. "I'm not doing this for sex."

Sandy raises an eyebrow as she stares back at me. "You sure about that?"

"One hundred percent," I say without my voice wavering, which is impressive since I'm not sure I'm telling the truth. And by the look on Sandy's face, she doesn't think I am either. "Okay. Okay. Maybe eighty."

She snorts. "Well, at least that thing isn't dead," she says as her gaze dips down my body. "I was starting to get worried."

"I'm here. I'm here," Mikayala says, running down the sidewalk in our direction. "Parking is a bitch around here."

"You should've met us at Iris's," Sandy tells her, having zero patience when it comes to Mikayla's ability to be on time—or, I should say, lack thereof.

Mikayla motions up and down her body. "This doesn't happen as quickly for me as it does you."

She is ridiculous. Mikayla is stunning and could easily go without makeup and still get hit on by plenty of men. She has a big chest, a flat stomach, an ass you could rest a drink on, and the deepest green eyes. Absolutely stunning. She is her own harshest critic, though, and picks herself apart more often than I am comfortable with.

"We're here for Iris to land her man. Not you," Sandy tells her with a disapproving shake of her head.

"Just because she's here to get some dick doesn't mean I can't be too," Mikayla replies.

I groan loudly and stare up at the night sky. "I'm not here for dick."

Mikayla and Sandy laugh in unison as I roll my eyes.

"I'm not."

"Oh. Okay," Mikayla says as she reaches up to clasp my shoulders before spinning me around to face the door. "Then, in you go."

The city street is surprisingly quiet, but I don't realize it until I walk through the doors of the Hook & Hustle. Most of the people inside are staring at a professional basketball game on television and coaching from their seats at the bar.

"Men," Sandy mutters behind me. "There's a booth."

I barely see where she points as my gaze drifts behind the bar, where Brax is standing. He isn't looking in our direction because he's too busy talking to a beautiful woman sitting at the opposite end.

"Damn. He's better in person," Sandy whispers in my ear before giving me a nudge forward.

My feet move, finally feeling like they aren't stuck to the floor by his presence. "I know," I say on an airy breath as I follow Mikayla to the booth in the corner.

I try to take the side with my back to him, but Sandy isn't having it. She grabs me by the hips and pushes me toward Mikayla on the other side.

Mikayla stays standing, waiting for me to get in first. They're trying to hold me captive—or, at least, that's how it feels. I thought my best friends were supposed to have my back, not force me into something that could be another huge blow to my confidence. There is little left after Lucas, and I'm not sure a rejection from the hot bartender won't take the last remaining sliver.

"How's the food?" Sandy asks as she grabs the menus from the condiment caddy on the table. "I'm starving."

"I didn't eat anything when I was here."

"I bet it's good," Mikayla says, swiping the menu from Sandy. "Italian bar has to have good food. It's impossible for it to be bad."

"Let's hope," Sandy replies as she stares down at her menu after taking it back from Mikayla's hands.

I study the menu like I'm going to have an exam on it in a few hours. I shift in my seat, hating the feeling of dread that's quickly taking root deep in my stomach.

"He's looking," Mikayla says. "Oh my God, he's so dreamy too."

Sandy glances over her shoulder as I peer up at her. "Damn, girl. If you don't make a move tonight, I may have to end our friendship to have a piece of him."

"You're gross," Mikayla tells her. "You'd never do that to our friend. You know she likes him."

"Then she better start acting like it," Sandy replies, giving my shin a kick under the table.

"He's coming. Shit. He's coming," Mikayla says quickly, her voice all high-pitched and nearly a squeal.

"Damn it," I whisper and take a few breaths, trying to get control of my anxiety.

"Iris." His deep, rich voice hits me, making the butterflies in my chest swirl into a full-on tornado. "What are you doing here?"

I glance up, meeting his dark eyes. "Hey." Somehow, my voice is strong and doesn't quaver as I take in his stunning smile.

"I'm Mikayla, her best friend, and she told us about this great bar, and we just had to see you...it... for ourselves." Mikayla gives Brax a sweet smile as I try to not choke on my own spit from her word slip.

Brax's smile widens. "I was hoping you'd come back," he says to me, completely ignoring Mikayla.

"You were?" I ask, shock filling my voice.

Sandy pats the pleather spot next to her in the booth. "Wanna sit?" she asks him. "I'm Sandy. The other best friend."

"Brax," he says to Sandy and then looks at Mikayla, finally acknowledging her. "It's nice to meet you both."

Mikayla doesn't seem fazed by the fact that a moment ago, he was so into me, he didn't even give her the time of day.

"You can sit," Mikayla tells him when he doesn't take the spot next to Sandy right away.

He pitches his thumb over his shoulder, but his

gaze is firmly planted on me. "The bar's busy, but I can get you guys some drinks to get started. And when it quiets down, if it does, I'll come sit for a few."

"I'll take a Moscow mule," Mikayla tells him.

"Cosmo," Sandy orders as an homage to our favorite television series.

"Beer," I say to him.

"You sure about that?" he asks me.

I nod. "One beer won't hurt."

Mikayla and Sandy stare at me, and I can almost see the wheels inside their heads turning after that tiny exchange.

"You got it," Brax says. "I'll be right back."

When Brax is a few feet away, Mikayla shoulder checks me. "What was that?"

"What was what?" I reply, playing dumb.

"He knows what alcohol does to you?"

I had left that part of our evening together out of the conversation I had with them. I knew they'd read too much into it because they already had us in a long-term relationship in their heads.

"We did shots."

Sandy glares at me. "And?"

I shrug. "I may have sleepwalked."

"And?" Sandy asks again.

"I may have curled up next to him."

Mikayla gasps. "How could you not tell us?"

"It didn't seem important."

Sandy scrubs her hands down her cheeks. "It didn't seem important."

"You snuggled with the man, and it didn't seem important?" Mikayla asks me, turning her body in the booth until she's facing me.

"I woke up in my bed alone. Nothing happened."

"Did he push you away?" Sandy asks, glaring at me.

"No. I don't think so."

"Girl," Mikayla says, drawing out the single word. "No man who isn't into a woman is going to let her snuggle up to him."

"He's just nice," I say, but when I glance in his direction, he's staring at me as he shakes what I assume is Sandy's cosmo.

I smile at him, and he smiles back, making me squirm.

"You really are an idiot. I take back what I said earlier," Sandy says to me as she shakes her head.

"You're giving him your number before we leave this bar," Mikayla tells me.

"What if he doesn't ask for it?"

"He's going to ask for it," she replies. "And if he doesn't, he's a bigger idiot than you."

"Yeah," Sandy adds. "The space between you two was crackling with so much electricity, I was worried I'd get shocked if I moved."

"You two are weird," I say, trying to bury my face in the menu.

"Here we go," Brax says, setting down Sandy's cosmo and then Mikayla's mule. "I brought you the lightest beer I could find behind the bar. Only three percent alcohol."

"Thank you," I say to him, taking the beer from his hands. "You're really sweet."

My fingers graze his skin, and if I didn't know any better, I'd swear the contact shocked me. But then again, it is winter and with the air being so dry, it happens often and when I least expect it.

"Just looking out for you. I wouldn't want you wandering off in your sleep tonight before I had a chance to take you out on a date."

Sandy and Mikayla both gasp, but thankfully, the sound is soft and hopefully quiet enough that Brax didn't hear it.

"Me?" I ask, tightening my hold on the beer bottle.

"Yeah, Iris. You." The soft smile on his face has my heart pitter-pattering a hundred miles an hour in my chest. "If you don't want to, though…"

"She wants," Mikayla says quickly, and it's my turn to knock my knee into her so she'll shut up.

"Sure," I answer.

"Sure," he repeats with a hint of laughter. "I'm almost wounded."

"No. Yes. I'd love to," I say.

It's now or never. I can't let Lucas's shit behavior ruin my entire life. He already screwed up the last handful of years. Brax is sweet and handsome. I should at least give him a shot, especially after the easiness of our conversation after the bar closed and the morning after at the apartment.

"Yeah?" he asks, his face so full of hope.

"Yeah." I smile up at him, hoping I'm not going to screw this up.

"Thank God," Mikayla whispers as she clutches her chest.

"Will we be needing chaperones?" Sandy asks, but again, I ignore her and so does Brax.

"I'll grab your number in a bit. Do you ladies know what you want to order?"

My stomach's such a mess, I opt for the giant pretzel with the beer cheese dip. Anything greasy could send me over the edge at this point. I am so nervous I'm afraid I won't be able to keep down much more.

Once we give him our order, he promises to be back soon to check on us. I sit there in shock, unable to say anything right away.

But as soon as he is back behind the bar, Mikayla is the first to speak. "Fuck me," she mutters. "I thought for sure you were going to screw that up."

"Me too," Sandy says, reaching into her purse for her phone. "But I'm proud of you."

"What if I mess this up?" I ask them. "I could mess this up."

"How would you do that?" Mikayla asks.

"I could say something stupid."

"I'm not sure anything you say would chase that man away. He is smitten. S.M.I.T.T.E.N," Mikayla says, being overdramatic like she usually is.

"No, he's not."

Sandy stares at me, and I can read her mind. I'm an idiot. "You're the smartest out of the three of us with some things and so damn dense about other things."

"I take offense to that."

"You would," Sandy says. "I agree with Mikayla. I never once saw Lucas look at you that way. Not for a single moment."

I don't answer right away. I think about what Sandy just said and how Brax looked at me. Did Lucas look at me the same way? Maybe. I blocked out so much of our time together after he shattered my heart into a million pieces. It is almost impossible to think about any happy times we had together after what he did to me. The way he hurt me. How he embarrassed me.

"Not all men are like Lucas, darling," Sandy says, reaching across the table to touch my hand. "You have to put yourself out there sometime, and I think Brax is the right person for right now."

"I've never been good at casual," I remind her.

"I know, baby. I know," Sandy says as she pulls back her hand. "Maybe it won't be casual. Maybe it will. Don't label things right now. You deserve a night out with a nice guy who's so handsome he could be a movie star. You deserve some laughs and some flirting."

"She deserves some heavy petting too," Mikayla adds with a giggle-snort.

Sandy nods. "A lot of heavy petting."

I sigh as I glance in Brax's direction. As soon as our eyes meet, he winks. Luckily, I'm not in the middle of swallowing my beer or I might have choked to death on the liquid.

"He's dreamy," Mikayla whispers.

"You two sound like you need to get laid more than me."

"Does he have an older brother?" Sandy asks. "Because you're right. I do. I deserve it too."

"He has a younger one."

Sandy wrinkles her nose. "I like my men more seasoned."

"Then you're shit out of luck."

"How young are we talking?" Mikayla asks. "I'm not as picky as her."

From her lips to God's ears. Mikayla is an equal opportunity dater and makes no bones about it. She's never been shy or embarrassed by anything. I love that about her too.

"I don't know exactly."

"Shame," she mutters against the rim of her mule.

The food arrives in record time, and Brax makes a point to bring it over personally. I haven't seen him wait on any other tables besides ours. He's too busy with the customers around the bar to wander into the main dining room. That means something, right? We're special in some way. Maybe Mikayla and Sandy are right. Maybe he is smitten with me.

"I'll be over for a bit once you're done eating. Hard to eat and talk," he says as he hands me the plate with a giant pretzel. "I gave you extra cheese dip."

I smile up at him as I take in the three small bowls on the plate, which I know is overkill, but I'm not mad about it. "Thank you."

"Smart man. The way to a woman's heart is always through melted cheese," Mikayla says as she grabs the ketchup bottle from the middle of the table.

"That's what my sister says too," he replies. "Be back in a few. Holler if you need anything."

"Thanks," I say again, not sure of what else there is to add.

"If you don't get naked with that man on your date, I'll be extremely disappointed in you," Mikayla says, using a French fry to point at Brax's behind. "I'd bite that. It's built for biting."

"I'm not a vampire."

"I didn't say drink his blood. Bite that ass, girl. Leave a mark."

I gawk at her, blinking a few times. "What?"

"Claim it."

"Who are you?" I ask her.

Mikayla tilts her head, studying his ass some more. "A woman who knows what she wants and how to get it. You either bite that ass or someone else will."

"You're seriously delusional," I mumble as I tear my pretzel apart and wonder... Do people really do that? "I would never. I couldn't."

"You better expand your horizons." Mikayla turns her head toward me, showing me her teeth before she snaps at me like a turtle. "If you want to own that ass, you got to claim it."

"I need new friends," I lie, because I know I have the two best friends in the world and all they want for me is the very best.

Although I have no plans to bite his ass, I know I want to see it...soon.

CHAPTER 7
BRAX

AT WHAT AGE does dating become hard or damn near impossible? I fear I am getting close to finding out.

Before Iris, I didn't put much thought into the actual act of dating. I winged the hell out of every bit, but then again, I was never truly into the girl I was taking out either.

If I'm honest with myself, dating was about sex.

But tonight's different.

I am at an age where I want more. After watching my sister fall in love with Wylder, I know I want that too. Not Wylder. Shiver. But someone who would be mine and have my back, no matter what happens.

Coming home to an empty apartment doesn't hold the same appeal it did five years ago. It isn't as exciting to have a place all to myself without other people around to interrupt whatever I'm doing, which usually involves my bed in some form.

Tate: Don't mess this up. Try not to talk too much.

I grunt at the phone screen as I read my sister's text in our cousins' group text, which is always a much different conversation from the group text I'm in with my parents and siblings.

Me: I'm charming.

At least, I can be when I want to be, and with Iris, I very much want to charm her.

She wanted to meet me at the restaurant. She wouldn't let me pick her up, making an excuse about Chicago traffic and how it would be easier to meet somewhere in the middle of the city.

The restaurant I chose is nice, but not the most expensive. My grandmother would call it swanky, but by no means is it top-tier in a city like this.

I glance down at my phone, hoping to see an update from Iris. But instead, I see my other cousin siding with my sister.

Lulu: You're not. I'm with Tate. Speak very little.

Me: Anyone going to back me up?

I wait, hoping someone sides with me.

Mason: Talk away, big bro. If she doesn't love your obnoxious attitude, then she isn't the girl for you.

Obnoxious. I'm not obnoxious. I am confident, and those words have two very different meanings. My brother is the one with the obnoxious attitude, not me.

Amelia: You really like this woman, huh?

Amelia's a good soul. She's sweet. There has always been a kindness about her. An innocence that seems to be lacking in the rest of us.

Me: I do…a lot.

Nino: You got this.

Amelia: Sending good vibes your way.

I smile at Amelia's and Nino's messages as the door opens and Iris walks in, looking more beautiful than ever before.

My breath lodges in my throat as time seems to slow. I can't take my eyes off her as the wind from outside whips around her before the door closes behind her. Her gaze doesn't find me at first as she smooths down her hair.

I smile as I rise to my feet from the restaurant's bar and head her way. "Hey," I say when I'm a few feet away.

Her face instantly softens as her eyes meet mine. "Hey," she says back. "The weather is so crazy."

"Wintertime isn't much fun," I tell her.

Besides the bitter cold and shorter days, the number of layers we need to wear is suffocating. There isn't one thing about the season that makes me happy.

"I almost didn't make it. My car is still acting weird."

"I know a guy who can look at it for you."

"I know a guy?" She snorts. "What a very Chicago thing to say."

I laugh, hating that she's right. Everyone around here knows a guy who can do or get anything, and I'm not an exception, but I'm also not special.

"Sir," the hostess says from behind her wooden desk. "Your table is ready."

"I'm starving," Iris says to me as she unbuttons her full-length wool coat that is probably warmer than anything I own.

"Let me," I say as I move behind her, helping her with her coat.

She doesn't say no and shrugs off the heavy material with such grace compared to the way I'd do it.

"I'll take that," a man says from behind me. "Here's the ticket."

"Swanky," Iris mutters, giving me a big smile. "I'm impressed."

It's not lost on me that she uses the same word my grandmother would. It's an old one and not something I hear often.

"Been here before?" I ask her, motioning for her to walk in front of me.

"No," she says as she follows the hostess into the main dining room, and I trail behind her.

My gaze travels down the back of her, taking in the tight fit of her dress and the way it hugs her hips and waist perfectly.

The hostess stops in front of the best table in the place. "Is this to your satisfaction?" she asks.

"Better than I could've expected," I tell her as I move to pull out Iris's chair for her.

The table is next to the fireplace, giving us much-needed heat and ambiance. I set it up that way since my good friend from high school owns the place. He did me a solid with this last-minute booking, and I owe him one for it.

"Impressive." Iris smiles up at me as she takes the seat.

"Which part?" I ask as I sit across the table from her.

"Your manners and the table."

"The manners were hammered into me at a young age, and the table... I know a guy."

She laughs as she takes the menu from the hostess's hand.

"The chef would like to make a special meal for you, but if you'd prefer to order off the menu, he'd be happy to do that too," the hostess says. "He'll be out shortly to say hello, Mr. Gallo."

"I guess you do know a guy." Iris smiles as she looks down at the menu, her face illuminated by the fire.

"I know a lot of guys," I tell her, studying the soft lines of her face.

She glances up, catching me staring. "How do you know him?"

"We went to school together. He grew up in the neighborhood."

"I only keep in touch with Sandy and Mikayla from school. I couldn't even tell you where everyone else went. High school ended, and everyone scattered."

"That's a shame."

"Not really, if you knew the snooty people I went to school with." She laughs. "They were awful."

"Northsiders," I whisper.

"We're not all snobby."

"You aren't and neither are your friends, but the rest…" I can't take my eyes off her as she looks down at the menu. How did I get so damn lucky? It's like the snowstorm was sent on purpose to throw us together. Maybe winter will end up being my favorite season after all.

"I bet you secretly love the Cubs."

"I would be kicked out of the neighborhood if I loved the Cubs."

She snorts. "Liar."

"Braxton," David says as he comes to stand beside our table.

I instantly rise, giving my old friend a hug… something that isn't abnormal in our neighborhood. "Good to see you, man. This is Iris."

David's eyes light up as he drinks in Iris. He's as smitten as I am with her beauty. "It's my pleasure," he says with a tip of his head. "I hope you're comfortable at this table."

"It's perfect," I tell him, because it is. I couldn't have picked a better spot for a first date. It is romantic and private, but not too over the top.

"Your restaurant is beautiful," Iris says to him as I ease myself back into my seat.

"Thank you. It's been a labor of love, but I could've never imagined it would be as popular as it's been."

"He's being modest. David's the best chef I know."

David chuckles. Modesty has never been his strong suit. We have that in common, along with other things. "So, this evening, I would like to prepare something special for the two of you. Is that good?"

Iris nods and I say, "Yes."

"Great. Any food allergies?"

I shake my head as Iris replies, "No."

"Excellent. I'll send out the first course soon, and if you need anything, please ask Eileen to get me. She'll be your server this evening."

"Thank you," I say to David, extending my hand.

"Anything for you, Brax," he says before turning his attention toward Iris. "He's a good guy. Sometimes his mouth gets him in trouble, but he's a good one."

Iris snorts. "I'll make a mental note of that."

"Back to the grind," David says before leaving the table and heading toward the back of the restaurant.

"He seems nice," Iris says when he finally disappears into the kitchen.

"He is now, but he was wild when we were in high school."

"We all had our moments," she replies.

I tuck that nugget away, wondering what she did in high school that she'd classify as wild. I can't imagine her doing anything dangerous or out of the norm. She doesn't seem the type.

"You've had his food before?"

I nod. "He worked at the bar while he was attending culinary school here in the city. I was sad to see him go, because the man made the best burger I've ever eaten in my life."

"Good evening," a woman says as she comes to a stop at the side of our table. "I'm Eileen, and I'll be taking care of you. Chef has gifted you a bottle of our best champagne." She shows me the bottle, but I wouldn't know a good champagne from a bad one even if it hit me upside the head. "Is this to your liking?" The question is directed at me. If David says it's good, then it has to be.

"Yes," I tell her.

She sets down two glass flutes and goes to work filling them.

"Do you like champagne?" I ask Iris.

"Of course, but I don't have it often because..." She smiles.

"One glass," I tell her.

"Only one."

"Your first course will be out shortly."

I lift my flute, and Iris does the same. "What should we toast to?" I ask her as the flames lick the side of her face, creating a beautiful glow in her eyes.

"To new beginnings," she says, and my insides become warmer than the fire next to us.

"To new beginnings," I repeat, clinking my glass against hers.

We stare at each other over the rim of the glasses, taking our time savoring the champagne. I try not to make a face, but the liquid is so bitter, it's hard not to spit it out.

"Wow, that's…" Iris's voice trails off.

"Sour," I finish.

She chuckles as she sets the flute back on the table. "We won't have to worry about me having more than one glass. It's too tart for me."

I lean forward, clasping my hands together. "I need to be honest with you."

She mimics me until our faces are only a foot apart. "What is it?"

"I liked when you snuggled against me."

Her face turns a bright shade of pink. "Can I be honest too?"

"Yeah," I say softly.

"I wish I remembered because I'm sure I liked it

too." She eases back into her chair, never taking her eyes off me.

"Well, damn," I mutter. "We could do it while you're awake, and you can find out."

She smirks, and for a moment, I think I've gone too far until she says, "We may have to do just that."

I'm stunned into silence. Something that doesn't happen to me often. I compose myself as I lean back, staring at her. "Really?"

When did I become the type of man who got excited about snuggling? It isn't me. Never has been. But there is something about Iris that makes me want to get closer, even if it is only cuddling. She has a shit past, and I'll take whatever type of touching she is comfortable with. I only know I want whatever she is willing to give.

"We'll see. So far, my answer is yes."

So far... "I won't fuck it up," I promise her.

Iris laughs, and it's the most beautiful sound in the world. "I have faith in you."

"Here we go," Eileen says, interrupting our moment. "The first course features bacon-topped deviled eggs on a fried tomato base with house-made garlic aioli."

My mouth instantly waters at the sight of them as she sets the plate on the table. "Damn," I whisper, trying not to drool on myself.

"These look amazing," Iris tells Eileen.

"They're my absolute favorite," Eileen replies. "Would you like anything else to drink?"

"Water, please," Iris says.

"Make it two, please," I tell Eileen before she leaves.

"I don't think I've ever had anything like this before. I'm excited to taste it," Iris says to me as she lays her napkin across her lap.

"Me too," I say as I stare at her, but I'm not talking about the food in front of us.

Iris catches my eye, and when her cheeks turn pink again, I figure she's reading all my dirty thoughts.

"And I don't think it will be the most delicious thing I taste tonight either." I'm feeling her out now. I want to know how timid she is or how against sex she is after her douchebag ex left her. Maybe, just maybe...

"I hope it's not," she fires back without missing a beat.

"I plan to savor every single bite."

She visibly swallows as her breathing quickens. "Oh."

I smile at Iris, wishing I could reach across the table, grab her face, and taste her lips. Why I didn't ask for a booth or to sit next to her is beyond me. As my sister would say... I'm a dummy.

I grab the utensils and scoop up an egg with a tomato, holding it over Iris's plate. She hasn't taken her eyes off me, though. "Do you want?" I ask, staring back at her with as much heat building inside me as the fire next to us.

"Yes," she says, her voice all breathy.

And I know in this moment, neither of us is really talking about the damn eggs.

CHAPTER 8
IRIS

MY PHONE BUZZES in my purse for what feels like the hundredth time since I sat down at the table.

"You want to check that?" Brax asks as he pushes his empty plate to the side of the table.

"No," I tell him, but the sheer frequency has me worried that something is wrong.

"My phone hasn't stopped vibrating in my pocket."

"Really? It seems we're both in demand tonight." I smile at him, wondering if the night is almost over.

"My family is nosy."

"That's how my friends are," I explain as I set my fork down on my plate, unable to finish another bite.

"I like them."

"My friends?" I ask him.

He nods. "The two you were at the bar with were great. They really love you."

My insides warm at the information I already knew. They'd jump in front of a bullet for me. I had to beg them not to go after Lucas and castrate him, because I like having them around and didn't want them to go to prison for me. He wasn't worth it. "They're pretty great, but they're nosy and bossy."

Brax chuckles. "It could be worse, yeah? No one could care about either of us. I guess we're lucky."

I laugh softly as I wipe my mouth. "I don't know if it's luck. Sometimes they go a little too far."

David approaches the table, throwing a dish towel over his shoulder. "Was everything good?"

"Good?" I say, giving him a big smile. "It was one of the best meals I've ever eaten."

David tips his head to me. "You're very kind and beautiful."

Suddenly, I hear a low rumble coming from Brax's side of the table. I drag my gaze to him, and he's staring daggers at David.

"No worries," David says to him. "Don't get your hackles up, buddy. I know she's yours."

My eyebrows pinch on their own as I stare across the table at Brax. She's yours. What in the world?

"This is our first date," I blurt out for some reason, not thinking before speaking.

David's eyebrows rise. "Really?"

"Don't even think about it, David," Brax warns him, showing me a side of him I haven't seen before.

David laughs as he touches Brax's shoulder. "I'm married now, Brax. Relax. Down, boy."

Brax pulls in an audible breath as I sit here confused as hell. Where did this side of him come from? It is a little more aggressive than I've seen him before, but I'd be lying if I didn't admit that a part of me likes it.

Lucas never made a point of letting anyone know I was his. Looking back on it now, I know it had less to do with me and more to do with him. He was still playing the field, while I thought we were in a committed relationship. He didn't want anyone to know his dating status because he was always on the lookout for his next lay.

"You're lucky I love you like a brother," Brax tells David. "You did that shit on purpose."

David slaps Brax's shoulder playfully. "Maybe. I always like to see how you'll react, and that reaction was very telling."

"Asshole," Brax mutters, to which David laughs again.

"Dessert?" David asks, ignoring Brax's comment.

"I couldn't," I tell him. "Everything was so good. I should've stopped eating halfway through my meal."

"I'll have something wrapped up for you two to take with you. Good?" he asks Brax and not me.

"Yeah. You're a good man, David, even if you still like to test my patience."

"Give me a call sometime. Maybe we can double-date," David tells Brax before the two of them shake hands.

"I'll do that."

"I hope to see you again," David says to me with a spark in his eye.

"Maybe," I tease, but I hope to see him again soon too.

Not because I'm interested in David, but I really like Brax. Even though his name sounds like a dinosaur, Braxasaurus-Rex has my belly flipping out of lust, not fear.

"Work your magic," David says to Brax before wandering away.

"Maybe?" Brax asks with one eyebrow raised.

I laugh, liking his playfulness. "The night hasn't ended yet. There could be some major disaster."

"Like what?"

I stare at him across the table, wondering how much fire I want to play with. My body makes the decision before my mind has a chance to stop my mouth from opening. "Maybe you're an awful kisser."

I think he's going to give me a light response or laugh, but again, my mind isn't firing on all cylinders.

Brax leans forward, his upper body covering half the table. He brings his face close to me and stares me straight in the eyes, no hint of a smile on his lips.

There's a seriousness around him that makes the air heavy, and suddenly, it's hard for me to breathe.

"Are you ready to find out?"

I gulp, almost swallowing my tongue. Do I want to find out? Heck yeah. My body's been ready since the moment I walked into the restaurant. But my lips haven't touched another's in over a year. What if I'm the bad kisser in this situation?

"Um," I mumble, at a loss for words.

"Cat got your tongue?" he says with a hint of a smirk.

Staring into his eyes, I feel my heart race uncontrollably as my stomach twists and turns in anticipation. "No."

"No?" He leans closer, and the smirk from a moment ago is gone. "No, you don't want to find out, or no, a cat doesn't have your tongue?"

This is it. This is my chance to take the lead, something I've never really been good at with the opposite sex. I stand and turn my gaze toward him. "You comin'?" I ask, throwing him a more sinful smirk than he gave me a moment ago as I shrug on the coat that's just been brought to me, along with our to-go desserts.

He rises from his chair immediately, grabs his jacket, and takes a step toward me. I instantly move, heading right for the door. I don't look back as I slip outside, the cold air almost sizzling against my overheated skin.

I don't make it two more steps before Brax grabs my arm and spins me around. Without saying a word, he pulls me flush against his body as his eyes search mine. Snow falls around us like something out of a fairy tale. The city noise dampens like we're in a private bubble no other sound can penetrate besides our labored breathing.

"You want this?" he asks, his eyes scorching into my soul.

"Yes," I breathe, unable to do anything else.

My body's yearning for his touch. It's been far too long since I've felt a burning need inside me, and it's so intense, I wonder if I'll spontaneously combust if he doesn't press his lips against mine.

The worry vanishes when he takes my mouth hard and fast as he slides his hand up the back of my neck, tangling his fingers in my hair. Every nerve ending in my body that has been dormant for years suddenly comes alive.

My body melts against his, wanting his warmth and craving the hardness of him. My mind is filled with thoughts, but nothing is processing because I'm too lost in the roughness of his kiss.

I press my palms against his stomach, moaning as his teeth nip at my bottom lip before his tongue slips into my mouth, dancing with mine. I trace the lines of his abs with my fingers as I move my hands to his back, trying to find a way to tether myself to him…to this moment.

My toes curl in my boots, something I've never experienced before. Everything feels new and different from the past. Is it because it's been so long or because it's him? I don't have time or the ability to decide because he moves one hand up to my face, cradling my jaw in his warm palm. I open my lips wider, letting his mouth have free rein over mine.

And just as quickly as it began, the kiss ends. He pulls away, leaving me panting for more.

"Your place or mine?" I ask, not ready for the night to be over. This is a different side of me, and if I don't act on it, I'm not sure I'll ever be this bold again.

Brax sweeps his tongue across his bottom lip, and my knees wobble at the memory of how he tasted. "My truck," he says as he grabs my hand, pulling me down the sidewalk. "There's no time to drive anywhere."

"No time for what?" I follow him, letting him lead me toward his truck.

"I need more."

"I've never done it in a car," I blurt out, and I almost trip as the realization of what I just said crashes over me.

Brax stops abruptly and turns to face me. "We're not doing it in the car, Iris." He shakes his head and smiles down at me. "I'm not that kind of guy, but I want to kiss. I want to touch you, and I don't want to wait."

"We're not going to do it?" I ask, confused.

He shakes his head again. "Not yet."

Part of me is crushed by his statement. It has been far too long since I've had an orgasm that wasn't of my own making, and I was looking forward to seeing if Brax had the ability to give me one. I have full faith that he has the skills, and probably the experience, to make it the best one of my life.

I haven't made out in a car since high school, but if that's what Brax wants to do, I am all for it. Kissing and heavy petting will be the perfect way to end this evening until he's ready for more. Maybe I'm not what he expects or wants, but he's willing to give me a little more to remember him by.

But as soon as my feet come unstuck from the snow and my body moves with his, I remember he said not yet. That gives me hope. Maybe I won't have to memorize every moment I'm about to experience to last me until the next time I see some action.

When we round the side of the restaurant and walk into the parking lot, I see a truck that's idling in its parking spot.

"I heated it up already," he says as we approach the beast. "I don't want you to be cold."

I don't bother telling him it would be impossible for me to get hypothermia with the amount of heat coming off my body from need. He opens the door for me, something that still makes my heart skip a beat. The man has old-school manners, and every minute I'm with him, the more points he gets in the perfect date column.

"In you go," he says as he opens the door and waits for me to climb inside.

I take his hand as I step onto the running board and situate myself in the front seat. I glance around and am happily surprised that it's a bench seat. Making out wouldn't have been possible in my sedan because the middle console would be in the way, but this...this was made for action.

Maybe I'm not the first woman to be in this position either, but as soon as that thought enters my mind, I push it away.

It doesn't matter what's happened in the past. The only thing that is important is this moment, and I am going to do my best to live it to the fullest.

The windows to the truck are blacked out, giving us much-needed privacy for what I hope is about to happen.

Brax opens the door to the driver's side and sloughs off his coat, throwing it behind the seat before he climbs in. "Take it off," he says as his eyes drop to my long wool coat. "It'll be in the way."

I don't argue because he's right. And the last thing I want is something in the way of whatever he's about to do to me. I slide my arms out of the jacket and push the bulky fabric down behind me.

He presses a button on the dashboard, and the

steering wheel moves farther away from him. "Come here," he says, patting his lap. "Climb on top."

I nearly swallow my tongue at the thought of sitting in his lap. The only thing that would make it better would be if we were naked. I'd give an appendage to feel his hot skin flush against mine.

"My dress." I glance down, suddenly hating my fashion choice. I wanted him to see my body, but the tight fit of the material makes it impossible for me to swing my leg over his.

"Pull it up."

I grunt in frustration. Men. It's not that damn easy to bunch up a dress to my hips when I virtually had to squeeze my body into the fabric. "But…"

"All the way up. No one can see."

I glance around, and my eyes catch on the front windshield. We're facing the side of the brick building. There isn't a window in the truck through which anything would be visible to anyone in the outside world. On top of that, it's dark outside and there's barely any light inside the cab of the truck besides the faint glow from the dashboard.

I immediately go to work on shimmying the bottom of my dress almost all the way up my hips until my legs have free movement. I'm in his lap a moment later, straddling him.

As I settle, I drag my gaze to his face, finding him staring at me with fire in his eyes.

"Good?" he asks.

"Good," I reply before he moves his hand to the back of my neck, pulling my face toward his.

I place my hands on his shoulders, closing my eyes as our mouths meet, the fireworks from earlier sparking back to life behind my eyes.

My body slides forward, my aching center pressing against his hard, fabric-covered length. I moan at the contact, wanting more.

Again, I lose myself in the feel of his lips against mine. The hardness of the kiss that I crave like it's my lifeline to this universe.

He settles his warm palm on my hip, gripping me roughly as he digs his fingers into the fabric bunched around me.

"What do you want?" he asks against my mouth.

"You," I breathe in response.

"You want to come, baby?"

"Yes," I moan, pressing my middle harder against his cock.

"Ride me," he murmurs before kissing me deeper than before.

I move slowly at first, rocking my body forward in long, slow movements as his tongue tangles with mine where our mouths are connected.

The feel of his cock is overwhelming against my sensitive skin that's covered only by a pair of silk panties I wore in case I got lucky tonight. I can't stop the pressure building inside me from coming on too fast and strong. That's what I get for going years without the feel of a man against my skin.

I'm panting into his mouth, moaning as an orgasm crashes over me out of nowhere. He digs his fingers deeper into the meat of my hip, almost to the point they'll leave a mark. But I can't complain. The mix of pain and pleasure is absolutely perfect as I grind against his dick like my very life depends on it.

Brax moans as my movements slow and the orgasm starts to wane. "Fuck," he groans against my lips. "That was…"

"Too fast," I answer for him as I pull away from his mouth, trying to catch my breath.

"I was going to say hot."

I laugh, suddenly overcome with feelings and sensations. "Oh."

His fingers tighten behind my neck as he pulls my face closer. "I'm not done." I gasp as he moves his hand from my thighs to my damp panties. "We're just getting started, baby."

CHAPTER 9
BRAX

"WELL, I guess the date went well," my sister says as she pours herself a cup of coffee behind the bar. "I haven't seen you smile this much in…"

I keep my eyes down, finishing a crossword puzzle I've been working on for the last hour. "Don't you have a shop to open?"

The bar is nearly empty, with only a few regulars who should have their names imprinted on their stools. It's the same thing every day. I open the bar, and they file in to shoot the shit about nonsense while sipping their beers. Once all the drinks are poured, I lean against the bar and work on a crossword puzzle to pass the time before the lunchtime rush begins. From that moment on, the bar is busy until close.

"It's early." She leans next to me, getting into my personal space.

"Great," I mutter.

"Tell me about last night." She pumps my arm, nearly causing me to miss the square with my pencil.

"It was a date."

I know I'm not getting out of telling her details, but that doesn't mean I'm going to make it easy on her.

"I'm here. I'm here," Lulu says as she busts through the door and power walks toward the bar. "What did I miss?" she gasps for air, clearly out of breath from her quicker-than-normal pace.

"Nothing yet." Tate takes a sip of her coffee, making the most annoying slurping sound in the world. She knows it drives me crazy, and she has every intention of using it as a weapon against me in this conversation.

"Good. Good." Lulu climbs onto the stool in front of us and touches her chest. "Does the cold always make it so much harder to run, or is it just me?"

"That wasn't running," I tell her, not looking up from my newspaper.

"It was to me. I only have two speeds."

"Slow and slower," I tease before she has a chance to finish her statement. I love my cousin, but I swear her ass could be on fire and she wouldn't move any faster.

"Life isn't a race," she tells me.

"So..." Tate bumps into me again. "Spill the details, little brother."

I sigh deeply as I peer over to where she's perched. "What do you want to know?"

"Did you kiss?" Lulu blurts out.

Tate giggles. "That, but also, was it good? Are you going to see her again? Did you spend the night together?" she rattles off a few more questions, but I tune her out because my head is already swimming with too much overstimulation.

"All of that," Lulu adds.

"The date went well. Conversation was easy. I did not make an ass of myself."

"Shocker," Tate whispers under her breath, but I ignore her and keep on going.

"We did not spend the night together, and yes, we kissed."

"Ooooh," Lulu sings. "Hot."

"You kissed her on the cheek or the lips?"

Man, my sister is nosier than usual. I mean, she always wants to know everything, but today, she's extra pushy and ignores all the boundaries.

"I don't kiss-and-tell," I explain, dragging my gaze back to the crossword puzzle.

Before I can put my pencil against the paper, Tate swipes it off the bar top. "I'm not asking for a play-by-play," she says as she holds the newspaper ransom in her hand. "I don't want to know everything, but tell me, did you at least kiss her on the mouth?"

"Yes," I grumble.

Lulu and Tate squeal in unison.

"Did your toes curl when you did?" Lulu asks.

My eyebrows draw inward in an instant. "What?"

Lulu smiles at me, waggling her eyebrows. "You know."

"No. I don't."

Lulu rolls her eyes and shakes her head as she lets out a disgusted noise from deep in her throat. "Was the kiss so good that your toes curled in your shoes?"

I blink a few times, wondering what kind of drug she's on. "That shit doesn't happen."

"Uh. Yeah, it does," Tate tells me. "Wylder totally made my toes curl."

"That's a woman thing."

Lulu clears her throat and makes a funny face. "Sorry, bro. I mean, did she make your dick hard?"

I scrub my hand down my face, wondering what I did in life to deserve these two and this extreme line of questioning. "You two seriously need to get out more or find some friends."

"That's a yes and, also, so darn gross," Tate says. "In my mind, my brother is more like a Ken doll. Totally androgynous."

"Samesies," Lulu says to Tate.

"When are you seeing her again?" Tate asks me as I swipe the newspaper from her grip.

"Tonight," I tell her as I go back to figuring out the last word, and their line of questioning isn't helping my concentration.

"Excellent," Tate says. "We should double-date."

What is it with everyone and double-dating lately? I do not ever remember a time in my life when I've had it brought up twice in a matter of twelve hours.

"Why?" I ask her, but I don't hate the idea. It would take the pressure off me and let me see a different side of Iris than I've seen before. Tate has a way of bringing out the best in people, but also the worst.

"It would be fun. I could use a night out, and so could Wylder. I'd love to get to know my future sister-in-law."

My eyes widen for a split second as my heart stutter-steps in my chest at the very thought of getting married. "You're getting ahead of yourself, sis."

"I'll remind you that you said that the day you propose."

"What makes you think she's the one?" I ask her.

Tate throws her arm around my shoulders. "Because you always kiss-and-tell, and if you aren't telling, it's because you know there's something there."

"You're reading way too much into it."

"We'll see," she tells me. "You said you wanted to settle down, and then boom, a beautiful and available woman lands in your lap."

"It's like you ordered her straight from heaven," Lulu says in a dreamy voice.

"Don't you two have things to do?" I ask.

"I'm off today," Lulu tells me. "I thought I'd come here and reorganize the stock room."

"Clearly, you're normal," I tease her. "That's everyone's dream on their day off from their job."

"Babe, come organize my stock room across the street. It's a mess."

"I can do both," Lulu tells Tate.

"Totally normal," I mumble.

"Hey, if I didn't do it monthly, you wouldn't be able to find anything back there."

She's not wrong. It saves me hours of work every month, and for that, I'm thankful. People put things everywhere and ignore the labels that Lulu so carefully placed on every shelf.

"You're right," I tell her, giving her a small smile because the last thing I want is for her to leave. "I'm sorry."

She instantly perks up, giving me a bigger smile back. "I know you love me."

"More than Tate," I tell her, earning myself a pointy elbow right under my ribs.

"Jerk," Tate says.

Lulu hops down from her stool and grabs her purse off the bar. "I'm going to get started. I'll be listening to an audiobook, so if you need me, I won't hear you if you call."

"Got it," I tell her as she waves at Tate and me.

"See you in a bit," Tate tells her before she slurps her coffee again.

"You need to find her a man or a different hobby," I tell my sister when Lulu disappears in the back.

"That's no lie. She needs a man yesterday."

"Is she seeing anyone?"

"She's on hiatus."

"She's on hiatus?" I ask, because I'm confused, but that's my normal state around the two of them.

"She said she was taking a break from men this year. I'm hoping January is her month to shine."

"That worked out well for you when you did the same thing," I remind her.

"Hey, Brax. Can I get a refill?" Marvin, one of our regulars, asks.

"Yeah, bud," I tell him, moving to his empty pint glass.

"When the time is right, she'll find the one. You and I are proof of that," she tells me.

I glare at her as I refill Marvin's beer. "Again, I'm proof of nothing."

Tate grins as she finally puts her coffee cup in the sink under the bar. "Uh-huh."

"Whatever," I mumble as I set the beer down in front of Marvin.

"You getting married?" Marvin asks.

"No," I say at the same time Tate says, "Eventually."

"No, Marvin. I'm not getting married anytime soon. I went on a date last night."

"Good for you, kid," Marvin says as he lifts his beer glass up to his lips.

"What happened?" Clyde, Marvin's brother and our newest regular, asks as he slides onto the stool next to him.

"Nothing," I tell Clyde.

"The kid went and got himself a girlfriend," Marvin explains.

"Nice," Clyde says, lifting the beer to me that I just set in front of him. "I hope you have better luck with women than I do."

Marvin smacks his arm, nearly making him spill his beer. "Look at the man. Of course he has better luck than you and I ever could."

"My life would've been so much better with his body," Clyde says.

"You'd need his face too," Marvin says to Clyde. "Because yours is not that." Marvin points a finger at me.

"Mine's not bad," Clyde argues.

"It's not good either."

Clyde gives Marvin the middle finger.

"They're the best," Tate says at my side, but she's looking at them. "Don't be too hard on yourselves. You are two good-looking fellas."

"Liar," Marvin mutters against the rim of his glass.

"Told you," Clyde says, looking satisfied with himself.

"She's being nice, dummy," Marvin says to Clyde.

"Well, I have to go open the shop. What time are we meeting?" she asks as she walks toward the doors.

"Meeting?"

"For our double date."

"Damn," I whisper. "I'll talk to Iris and get back to you."

"Don't forget," she calls out as she leaves.

———————————

Ten hours later, Tate and Iris are laughing beside the fireplace at one of our favorite bars.

"No, he didn't." Iris covers her mouth to dampen her laughter as her eyes brim with unshed tears.

"Yes, girl. He so did."

Tate's telling Iris the story of how I broke my arm when I was sixteen. I always did ridiculous things when I was younger, and it's a miracle I somehow survived those years.

"Boys are so dumb," Tate adds.

"Hey now," Wylder warns playfully as he slides his arm across the back of Tate's chair. "What fun would we be if we didn't do crazy things sometimes?"

"Thank goodness we have girls," she tells him.

"Because they're the bastion of sanity."

"Maybe not, but I understand them better."

"Well, hopefully that one—" Wylder's eyes dip to

my sister's stomach "—will be a boy so you can better understand how we function."

My eyes widen as Tate's head swivels toward Wylder with the meanest glare I've ever seen her give anyone, and I've seen some doozies. "Wylder."

"Wait. Are you…?" I ask, not finishing the sentence.

Tate's face softens as she looks across the table to me. "It's not official yet. I just took the test this evening at home, and it was positive. But I have to schedule an appointment at the doctor to be sure."

"Oh my goodness. That's so exciting," Iris says.

"We weren't telling people yet," she says, pointing that glare back at Wylder. "I thought we discussed this."

He shrugs it off like he's discussing the weather and not their agreement on telling everyone they're pregnant. "It's only your brother. It's not a big deal."

"But my brother has a big, big mouth, and he could tell everyone. What if I go to the doctor and they say it was a false positive, and by then, half my family is already planning my baby shower?"

"Then I'll have to work double time to put that baby where it belongs." Wylder smiles at my sister, looking pretty damn pleased with himself, but she isn't finding his statement cute.

"Don't tell anyone," she begs me once she finally drags her angry gaze away from him.

I lift my hands. "My lips are sealed. I can keep a secret, unlike some other people in this family."

"If you say one word, I'll—"

"I like my balls where they are," I interrupt her, knowing exactly how she'll threaten me. I've spent my life dealing with her.

"I was going to say I'd slurp every drink in front of you for the rest of my life."

I wince, hating that more than a one-time kick in the nuts. "You go for the jugular."

"Damn right," she says with a smile.

"The whole family is going to shit a brick," Wylder says, reaching his hand across to place it on Tate's stomach, but she bats it away.

"Blabbermouth," she mutters.

"Were you trying to get pregnant?" Iris asks her.

"Yes," Tate says. "I love Maddox and Hazel, but we wanted a little one running around the house."

"It's a boy," Wylder states with so much certainty, I almost believe him.

"I don't care, as long as the baby's healthy," Tate says.

"Will it be your mom and dad's first grandbaby?" Iris asks Tate.

I see a flash of pain in Tate's eyes. I know exactly where it's coming from too. No shade against Tilly, but Tate still has such vivid memories of our mother. There's always been a hole left by her death that can't be filled by anyone, even the best stepmother in the entire world.

"It would be the first," Tate tells her. "And the entire family is going to make me crazy about it too."

"Truth," I say, lifting my beer bottle and tipping it in her direction. "Better you than me."

"Do you want kids, Iris?" Tate asks her.

I continue drinking, but the question has me paying attention.

"Yes. I'd like a few someday, but I'm far off that point, because," Iris says, wiggling her ring finger at my sister.

"Well, you have my brother now, so maybe it'll be sooner rather than later."

I almost cough my entire mouthful of beer across the table, but I catch most of it behind my hand. Tate has lost her mind. I can now blame her equally big mouth as Wylder's on her pregnancy hormones.

"Well, I… Uh…" Iris stammers, looking like a deer in headlights.

"Tate, calm it, baby," Wylder tells her.

"Look at them," Tate says, waving her hand between Iris and me. "They're perfect together."

"It takes more than hotness," Wylder tells her, and somehow, he's become the sane one at the table.

Iris glances down before looking up at me, and I know it's my time to act. "Let us get to know each other first before you have us married off with kids running around the yard, sis. Okay?"

"Yeah. Sure," Tate says. "But I like Iris a lot."

"Thanks," Iris says in reply. "I like you too."

I nearly roll my eyes but keep that locked down so I don't get another death glare from across the table. I know it's time to change the subject.

"What are my favorite nieces doing tonight?" I ask.

"Baking cupcakes with Ma." Tate sighs as she leans back into her chair and against Wylder's arm. "Well, probably eating more than baking, but same thing."

"That would be the best way to spend the evening as a kid," Iris states, and that's no lie.

Some of my best memories from childhood are of the three of us baking late into the night as Tilly tried new recipes and flavor combos for the store while Dad worked at the bar. I was a happy little taste tester for her creativity.

"Hell, it's a great way to spend the evening as an adult too," Tate says. "I should've become a baker instead of opening a tattoo shop."

"You can't bake worth shit," I tell her, remembering the last cupcake she made that disintegrated in my palm like a pile of sand. "Tattooing is your calling."

"I'm not that bad."

I raise an eyebrow.

She chuffs and mutters, "Fine. I am that bad."

"How did you get into tattooing?" Iris asks her.

"My family owns a shop in Florida, and I spent a lot of time there. I fell in love with everything about it every time I visited."

Her visits usually involved running from someone and hiding to keep herself breathing, but she leaves that bit out. I guess, in the end, it all worked out. If that hadn't happened, who knows what she'd be doing now, but working at Tilly's bakery wouldn't have been her final destination because, again…she's awful at baking.

"Wow, I had no idea."

"Do you have any tattoos?" Tate asks Iris.

I let my eyes roam over her exposed flesh, but I see nothing.

"One, but it's hidden."

I suddenly have the urge to strip her bare to see exactly where it is.

"What is it?" Tate asks.

"It's stupid. A mistake I made when I was eighteen, but since I can't see it every day, I sometimes forget it's there."

That narrows down the location, and suddenly, my goal is to find out where it is.

"I can do a cover-up if you want, or someone else at the shop can. You shouldn't have something on your skin you don't absolutely love. Maybe it's time for a change," Tate says before taking a sip of her soda, and somehow doing it so quietly, I can't hear it.

"Maybe I will," Iris says.

That limits my time. I want to see the before. I want to find it. I want to know all the parts of her from before I met her, and finding that tattoo is first up on my list of plans for my time with Iris.

CHAPTER 10
IRIS

BRAX'S PLACE is nothing how I imagined. I
don't know why I thought it would have bare walls
with very little furniture. Most men I know aren't into
having much around their living space, but that is
mostly from the lack of creativity and design
knowledge.

"Wow," I say as I pull off my winter boots, leaving
them on the rug near the door. "This is…" I'm at a
loss for words, really.

"My sister and mom did it."

Ah. That makes sense. This wasn't done by him,
but he has no problem living in a space as warm as
this. The loft is homier than most I've been in, with a
few walls painted in the blackest black and deep
greens.

"It's beautiful."

The furniture is in rich wood tones, with leather

and light-colored boucle fabrics. It's a place I could live in and nest forever. *You're getting ahead of yourself, Iris.*

I step into the expansive place, my eyes drifting around as I try my best to soak everything in.

Brax moves toward the large kitchen area with the longest kitchen island I've ever seen outside of a commercial kitchen. "Want something to drink?"

"Yes," I say as I spin around, and my eyes catch on the floor-to-ceiling windows overlooking a lit-up downtown.

"I bought this place because of that view."

I'm seriously impressed. Not only because of the decorating, but also because he bought it. I've only been able to rent. The city is ridiculously expensive, and the longer I wait to buy, the higher the prices seem to go.

I can't take my eyes off the city, watching the lights twinkle like the stars in the sky above. "I would've too. I have a stunning view of my neighbor's brick exterior."

Brax hands me a glass filled with soda as he comes to stand next to me, but he's not looking at the view in front of us. I can feel the heat in his eyes without looking at him.

"How long have you been here?" I ask, suddenly nervous to be alone with him.

But I'm not nervous because I fear him. I'm scared of what this could lead to and the constant worry that he could break my heart the same way Lucas did.

"A few years," he says. His voice is soft and warm, sliding over my skin like a caress.

"The snow is getting heavier," I say, trying to make small talk. From the seventh floor of his building, the city looks so peaceful with the flakes fluttering through the air and falling to the ground below.

I hadn't planned on coming to his place after the bar, but the snow started coming down at such a rapid clip, we both decided it was the safest and closest place for me tonight.

Damn winter.

My phone rings in my purse, causing me to jump. I thought I had the damn thing on silent because Mikayla and Sandy had been blowing it up on my way to the bar.

"Sorry." I stalk toward my purse, which I left with my coat and boots near the door.

"It's okay. Get it."

"No. No. It's okay," I tell him as my fingers find the cool metal in the bottom of my purse. But whatever I was going to say dies on my tongue as I see the name on my phone. "Son of a…"

"Something wrong?" Brax asks.

I peer up at him, trying to keep my face impassive. "No one important." I hit the send to voice mail button on the screen, not wanting to talk to Lucas now or ever.

But as I start to throw my phone back into my purse, it rings again. Before it makes it to the second ring, I send it to voice mail again.

"You sure you don't need to get it?"

"Need?" I laugh sardonically. "No. I don't need to get it. They're not important."

"Lemme guess. The ex?" Brax says, like he's reading my mind.

My face must have given me away. "Yeah," I whisper.

"Want me to answer?"

My breath catches in my lungs as I think about Brax's deep voice being the one to greet Lucas. "No. I can talk to him another time, but I really don't want to hear from him."

"Still hurts, huh?" His face looks curious, but not the good kind. He's wondering if I still have feelings for the man who broke my heart.

"No. I'm over him. I have been for a long time." And what I'm saying is true. I no longer feel hurt because any love I had for Lucas has withered away along with the sadness. "I would just prefer he never called again. In my mind, he doesn't exist anymore."

"Harsh, but I love it," Brax says.

I give him a small smile. "I'm not usually a mean person."

My phone rings again, and I groan.

"Maybe it's important," he tells me as his eyes dip to my hand.

"It doesn't matter to me."

He holds out his hand, and I willingly give him the phone. He touches the screen, and there's nothing but panicked breathing on the other end.

"Iris?" Lucas's voice fills the expanse of Brax's place. "Are you there?"

"I'm here," I say as Brax opens his mouth and is about to answer for me.

"Listen, I'm in a bit of trouble…"

"I don't care," I tell him, staring at Brax's face.

He's taking all this much better than I would've if the roles were reversed.

"You need to care."

"Why?"

Brax ticks his head toward the leather couch behind us, and I follow him, needing to sit down for this brief conversation with a man I swore I'd never speak to again.

"I got in over my head. It's why I left."

I almost burst into laughter. Left? He didn't just leave. He didn't go out for a run to the grocery store. He left me standing at the altar in front of everyone we knew and loved.

"That was years ago," I say, trying to keep the bitterness out of my voice.

"I thought I had it under control, but it's not anymore."

Brax's eyebrows are drawn together as his gaze dips to the phone screen in his hand, which his fingers are wrapped around like a vise.

"Not my problem," I reply.

"It is, though. They're coming for you."

My heart stutters in my chest, and my eyes widen as Brax's gaze comes back to me. "What?"

"I messed up, and now you're at risk. They know about you. Watch your back. Don't trust anyone," he says, his words rushing out of him in a torrent.

"But I'm no one," I whisper. "I don't have anything to do with you, Lucas."

My head is spinning, and I can barely breathe. How is this man still messing up my life years later? I thought I broke free of him and all the ways he affected my world, but once again, he's trying to pull me back in and break me in an entirely different way.

"I'll get it straightened out, but it's going to take time," he adds.

"What did you do, jagoff?" Brax says, finally entering the conversation.

"Who is that?" Lucas asks like he has any right to know who's in my life.

"I asked you a question," Brax states, not giving me a moment to answer, which is nice. "What did you do, and who did you do it to?"

"I don't know who the fu—" Lucas starts, but Brax isn't having any of it.

"I'm going to give you one more chance to

answer, and then you're going to be running from two people, not just one."

I see Brax in an entirely new light. He's been so laid-back and easy every time we've been together, but he's got a temper simmering underneath the cool exterior.

"I borrowed money. A lot of money," Lucas replies softly.

"How much, and from whom?" Brax asks.

"Two mil from a guy I know."

Two million dollars? What the hell did he need two million dollars for? Lucas was a successful investor with a large client list. I can't imagine what he'd need that kind of bankroll for. None of it makes sense.

"What the hell did you need two million dollars for?" I ask, curiosity getting the best of me.

"That's not important," Lucas tells me.

Asshole.

"Who did you borrow it from?" Brax asks again through gritted teeth.

"A man named Malakai."

"Fuck," Brax mutters as he shakes his head. "I have Iris handled. She'll be fine. You…not so much," Brax tells him. "Don't call again. Iris wanted nothing to do with you before this, and now she really doesn't want anything to do with you. Forget she's alive. Forget this number, or else you'll be running from me too. Got it?"

"But I…" Lucas starts.

"Do we understand each other?" Brax states in such a steely voice, I sit up a bit straighter.

"Who is this?" Lucas asks.

"Another nightmare," Brax answers, tapping his finger roughly against the phone screen.

I sit in silence, unable to speak. A slight tremble overtakes my body.

Brax tosses my phone down on the couch between us before he reaches out, cupping my hands in his. "Don't worry, Iris. I got you," he says in a soft voice that almost makes me believe what he's saying is true.

"I…I can't believe this," I whisper, staring down to where our hands are connected.

"I know Malakai. He won't hurt you."

My gaze snaps to his. "You know him?"

Brax nods. "He's a neighborhood guy, and since I run the bar and my family has been in the area forever, I know almost everyone, especially someone like Malakai."

I try to process his words, but they don't seem to penetrate the way they should. "You know bad people?"

"Bartenders know everyone."

I blink, soaking in everything that was said on the phone and the words we're speaking to each other now. "But you said especially someone like Malakai."

"My grandpa wasn't always on the up-and-up."

"The up-and-up?" I ask, confused.

"He has an illustrious past."

"Oh."

"Between my gramps and me, we'll get it all sorted."

As I look into his eyes, I believe every word he's saying. There's a sincerity there that I never saw when I looked at Lucas.

"I can't believe this," I say, dropping my head forward and taking a deep breath.

Years. It's been years, and Lucas is somehow still finding a way to screw up my life. The ridiculousness of it all is almost laughable. Almost.

Brax squeezes my hands. "Hey."

I lift my head, bringing my tear-rimmed eyes back to his gentle face.

"I promise it'll be fine. This is Lucas's problem and not yours. I'll protect you."

"I guess it's a good thing I'm staying here tonight."

"I want you to stay until I have a chance to talk to Malakai."

"What?" I seem to be saying that word a lot, but it's all still so unbelievable to me.

"You can't go home until it's safe."

My stomach rolls at that word.

Safe.

I'm not safe. Or at least, I wouldn't be if I were home tonight.

What would I have done if Lucas had called while

I was home alone and dropped this bomb on me? I would've absolutely lost my mind.

"How long will that be?" I ask him.

"Hopefully I can get my gramps to track him down tomorrow. A day or two."

I glance around the beautiful loft, which doesn't feel as warm as it did before.

"But I..." The words die in my throat. I don't know what I was going to say. My mind is moving a million miles a minute, and processing isn't going so well.

Brax gently tugs my arms, making the rest of me move. As soon as I'm closer, he snakes his arms underneath my legs and pulls me into his lap like I weigh nothing.

I snuggle into him, resting my cheek against his chest.

"You're safe," he repeats.

Wrapped in his arms with his chin resting on the top of my head, I feel safe. I'm enveloped by him and the warmth of his body. Despite the fact that there's someone out there who's looking for me, I feel oddly at peace on his lap.

"For now," I whisper, closing my eyes.

If Malakai doesn't kill Lucas, I may for putting me through this after a handful of years of being apart.

"You have my family's protection now," Brax says quietly as he slides his hand against my back.

I suddenly feel as if I've walked onto the set of an

old mafia movie even though I never auditioned for the part.

"I'm sorry."

Brax pulls back slightly until our gazes lock. "For what?"

I shrug one shoulder, feeling so drained. "For dragging you into my mess."

"It's not your mess. It's his."

I can't look away. His deep, dark eyes have me in a trance. "Okay."

"I promise," he says, not convinced by my response.

"I can go somewhere else. I can go to Mikayla's or Sandy's."

"They may know about them and be watching their places for you."

"Crap," I snap, shaking my head at the thought of something happening to them.

"I'm too new for them to know about unless they followed you tonight, but since you're still breathing, I'm going to guess they weren't."

I blink a few times as fear grips me harder. "But they could've." My eyes move toward the floor-to-ceiling windows, feeling more exposed than I did earlier.

Brax leans to the side and grabs a remote from the side table. He stretches his arm out toward the window and presses a button. In an instant, black shades come down from the ceiling, covering the windows.

"Better?" he asks as he sets down the remote.

"This is so messed up."

"Hold on," Brax says, lifting his backside and fishing his phone out of his pocket.

"Who are you calling?"

"My grandpa."

"At this hour?"

I've lost track of time, but it's well after midnight. My grandparents would have been asleep for hours. They have the weird habit of going to sleep right after the sun sets and getting up as it rises. I don't understand it, but they say I will when I'm their age.

"He's a night owl, and he turns his ringer off when he goes to sleep. I won't wake him."

Brax hits the speaker button, holding the phone out between us as it rings.

"Brax?" A man's voice fills the air.

"Hey, Gramps. Whatcha up to?"

"Watching some crazy show on the tube. You?"

"On a date."

"Nice," his grandpa says. "What's wrong? You rarely call this late."

"Got a problem, Gramps."

A problem? First, it's not his problem. Second, it's a little bit bigger than a problem. A problem would be you ran out of sugar while trying to make cookies. Not having someone out there hunting your girlfriend. I shake my head at my own stupid thoughts. I'm not his girlfriend. I'm just a woman he's gone on two dates with and gave one amazing orgasm to.

"Shoot, kiddo. How can I help?"

Brax winks at me with a little smile, but I can't muster the same expression to give back to him. "You know Malakai?"

"Malakai McGowan?" Gramps asks.

"That's the one."

His grandpa whistles. "He's a doozy."

"I know, and I need a favor."

"Did you get yourself in trouble with Malakai? I thought I taught you better than that."

"No. No. Not me," Brax replies.

I feel a little better about the conversation now. At least Brax was taught not to get involved with men like Malakai. That means his grandfather doesn't get involved with them either.

"Thank goodness. Darn near gave me a heart attack," his grandpa says.

Well, that's not good. I mean, I knew Malakai had to be bad from Brax's response, but his grandfather's words only solidify the fear that's taken root deep in the pit of my stomach.

"What do you need?"

"Well, the girl I've been seeing—"

"You're seeing someone? Who?"

Brax rolls his eyes even though his grandpa can't see. "You'll meet her soon." He gives me a forced smile because this is awkward for both of us. "Anyway, her ex-fiancé got involved with Malakai. Took out a massive loan and then didn't pay."

"Same old story," his grandpa says.

"Yep. Well, her ex just called and said Malakai may come after her, but she's not in his life and hasn't been for years."

"What a dummy," his grandfather mutters.

"No truer words, Gramps."

"I'll put out a call to Malakai, but you need to hide her until I can get it sorted."

"She's at my place."

"Does he know about your place?"

"We're new. Second date."

"Started that relationship off with a bang, eh?"

"I hope not," Brax whispers. "Poor choice of words on your part, Gramps."

"Keep her there. Don't let her out of your sight until I can talk to Malakai."

I swallow hard, staring at Brax. I hate that I have to put him in this situation.

"I think it's safer for Brax if I went home," I say, finally speaking up. "I don't want to put him in danger."

"Sweetie," his grandpa replies, his voice so soft and sweet, a few knots in my stomach loosen, "you stay there with my grandson. If anyone can keep you breathing, it's him. You're not going to put yourself in danger because you think you're putting his life at risk. Brax can handle himself. He knows how to handle bad guys, and I'm guessing you don't, but maybe I'm wrong."

I hate that he's right. I don't know shit about protecting myself. Sometimes, when I feel a little uneasy about a situation, I'll slide a key between my two fingers, so if I need to punch someone, they get stabbed too. It's ridiculous because I'm pretty sure my punch wouldn't actually do enough damage to break the skin, but it makes me feel better, even if it's delusional.

"Fine," I say, my shoulders instantly slumping forward.

"Any cars on the street in front of your place?" his grandpa asks.

Brax rises from the couch and heads toward the windows, moving the shades to see the street below. "No one."

"It's too cold for them to be standing on the street. They probably don't know about you yet or else I would've gotten a call from Malakai. He owes me as much before he tries to put a cap in your ass."

I hang my head and rest my face in my palms, shaking my head back and forth. If Malakai doesn't kill Lucas, I sure as hell will when I get my hands on his scrawny neck.

"I think we're safe here. Go get some sleep and let me know what he says tomorrow," Brax tells his grandpa as the couch dips next to me.

"Sonny, I'm not going to bed for hours. What do you think I am?"

"Old," Brax says, but his voice is light.

I peer up as Brax winks at me.

"Idiot," his grandpa mumbles. "You go to bed."

"I plan on it," Brax replies with a smile as his eyes lock on me.

"That's my boy," his grandpa says. "Someday you'll be old like me, and your balls will hang to your knees and your dick won't work. Use it before you lose it."

My eyes widen, and I cover my mouth to stop the giggle that's ready to break free. His grandfather is a hoot. I hope I am able to meet him someday and thank him for his help—if I'm able to get through this situation and remain breathing.

CHAPTER 11
BRAX

I ROLL to my side and open my eyes. Iris is in my bed, staring at me. "Hi," I whisper, hoping my breath doesn't knock her out.

"Hi," she whispers back.

I tuck my hand under my head, wishing I could stay in my warm bed all day, but I know it'll never happen. "Can't sleep?"

"I slept."

"What time is it?" I ask her, not wanting to move.

"Noon."

I've slept later. If she weren't here, I'd probably go back to sleep, but I don't think it's in the cards for today. "Come here."

She slides across the bed, turning on to her side so her back is to my front. She sags against me the moment I set my arm over her middle.

"You okay?"

"I think so," she says.

"We're still alive." I state the obvious, but I think she needs the reminder that we're okay now and will continue to be. I have full faith in my grandpa to fix things with Malakai on her behalf.

"For now."

I tighten my arm around her. "For a long time, baby. Trust me."

"I'm sorry Lucas has given me trust issues. You've done nothing except be good to me."

Men like Lucas don't deserve to breathe. They spend their entire lives messing up other people's existences without thinking about how their actions will affect anyone except themselves. If I ever lay eyes on him, he may not be breathing for long.

"You're fine," I remind her because she apologized profusely last night, and I don't want to go down that path again. "I'm not anything like Lucas, and you'll realize that soon enough."

Her fingers find the top of my hand, and she rakes her nails over the tender skin, sending goose bumps up my arm. "I already know you're not anything like him. "

"Do you feel safe?" I ask against her ear.

"Yes," she breathes, her body slack in my arms.

I groan as the sound of my phone vibrating on my nightstand fills the silence in the room. "Who would call at this hour?"

"It's noon," she reminds me with a hint of laughter.

"It's my day off, and everyone knows I like my sleep." I keep my arm around her as I move our bodies to grab my phone. "Hello," I say into the phone, holding it against my ear.

"Brax," Gramps says, sounding way more awake and alert than I feel. "I made contact."

"Do you sleep?" I ask him.

"It's noon," he replies, repeating Iris's words. "Anyway, I talked to Malakai's number two. We have a private meeting with him tonight."

"In person?" I ask, a small lump forming in my throat. I thought a call would take care of it, but I should've known better. This is Malakai, and he likes to toy with everyone, even my grandfather.

"He never makes anything easy."

"I guess not."

"What happened?" Iris asks, and I pull the phone away, pressing speaker so she can hear our conversation.

"What time?" I ask him.

"Ten at his favorite pub."

"What?" Iris asks as she turns her body and face so she can see me. Her eyes are wide, and her breathing has grown more ragged.

"It's a good sign, doll," Gramps says to Iris, because I've never been his doll. That's always been reserved for the girls of the family. I'm kiddo or bud.

All the boys are. It allows him not to have to remember any names since there're more than a handful of us. "He agreed to a sit-down. He could've told me to kick rocks."

"But this isn't your problem," Iris tells him.

"It's not yours either," he replies, instantly making her mouth close. "But now, it's all of ours, though it won't be for long. Malakai and I have a long history. It wasn't always pretty, but we've been on solid ground for years. By tomorrow, this will all be a memory."

"More like a nightmare," Iris mutters softly.

"We'll swing by and pick you up," I tell him.

"Come at seven. Grandma says you need to bring your girlfriend over for dinner before I'm allowed to go."

"You told her?"

"Well, yeah. Duh. The woman knows everything."

"I'm sorry," I tell Iris with a pained expression.

"Sorry? Don't be sorry," she says with graciousness.

"There's nothing to be sorry about. Your gram makes the best eggplant parm in the city. Stop being so dramatic. It's dinner, not an engagement party," Gramps tells me. "Be here at seven."

"It's not going to take three hours to eat," I argue, but I know it's no use. If Gram says seven, it's seven.

"You tell her that. She's the boss, kiddo."

"I love eggplant parm," Iris says, taking it all in stride.

She may love the food, but she has no idea what she's walking into. Betty Gallo is going to be filled with questions, and if she likes Iris, she'll be planning our wedding before we even make it to the pub to meet Malakai.

"I have to go. Your gram wants me to take her to the store so she can start cooking. See you later."

"Bye," I say.

"Thank you," Iris calls out before my grandpa hangs up.

"You're most welcome, darling."

Darling's a new one.

"Oh. I forgot to tell you. Pike and Gigi are in town for the week. They're coming to dinner too."

Now, the darling comment makes sense. "Sounds good," I tell him before he disconnects the call.

"Who are Gigi and Pike?" Iris asks as she moves to a seated position on the bed next to me with her legs folded underneath her body.

"Cousins from Florida."

"Oh." Her eyebrows rise. "Is your family big?"

"Enormous, but don't worry. Some of the pressure is off with them there tonight. My grandma won't be able to question us relentlessly with witnesses."

"Stop," she says as she laughs. "You're making your grandma sound scarier than Malakai."

"I'm honestly not sure which one is scarier," I say, pulling her toward me. "Betty can be something else."

"I can take it."

I press my lips to her bare shoulder, wishing she weren't wearing an old tank top and shorts of mine that are way too big on her. Somehow, she looks good in the raggedy old clothes. "I'll remind you of that later."

"I need coffee," she says, killing any plans I have of having her for breakfast.

"I'll make a pot," I say against her shoulder, trying to keep the grumpiness out of my voice.

"Do you have good coffee?" She peers over her shoulder, her eyes meeting mine.

"I don't do half-assed coffee," I lie.

Yesterday morning, I picked up what my mom said were the best beans you can get at the grocery store. And since Iris loved the coffee at Tilly's bakery, I figured I'd listen to her advice. Before then, I did indeed have shit coffee in my cabinet, but Iris doesn't need to know that.

"Take your time getting up, and I'll get it started," I tell her, untangling my body from hers.

"I don't have anything to wear," she says as she rolls over, putting her palm under her head. Her eyes travel down the length of my body, and I can see the heat in her gaze. "I can't go to your grandparents' in this."

I grab a T-shirt from my dresser and pull it on, hating that I put the thermostat so low last night. I wanted her to come to me for warmth, and my plan worked perfectly. "I'll call my sister. She can bring some clothes for you to wear."

"You're too good to me." She stretches, and the tank top she's wearing rides up her stomach, exposing the skin I've been dying to taste.

"Never accept anything less, Iris."

"Okay," she whispers.

I smile, but my eyes are locked on the stretch of her exposed stomach.

"Coffee," she says when I don't move right away.

"Got it," I say, clearing my throat and spinning on my heel before my body decides to put on a show, giving away every dirty thought that's going through my head.

An hour later, Tate's at the kitchen island with a bag full of clothes for Iris to try on.

"So…" Tate says as she cups the hot mug of coffee in her hands. "Gram's tonight?"

"Yeah." I lean over the island, sipping on my second cup. "You two coming?"

"I think so. We have to see if Cheryl will watch the girls, but I'm pretty sure she's a yes."

"I could use some backup," I tell her.

"She can't be that bad," Iris says, entering the conversation about Betty.

Tate laughs and reaches out, patting Iris's hand. "She's not bad, but she's persistent—though, it's worth it for her eggplant parm. But don't eat anything else."

"Why?" Iris asks Tate.

"She's an awful cook, but thankfully, she can make eggplant like an expert."

"Really?" Iris asks, glancing between us.

"It's true," I tell her. "Eat only the eggplant."

"Okay. Well, I'm excited about it, but I wish we weren't going there for the reason we are," Iris says.

"I still can't believe it. Brax told me everything when he called, and I'm still in shock."

"I'm trying not to freak out," Iris tells Tate.

Tate lifts the mug to her lips, but before she takes another sip, she says, "Malakai is something else, but I know Gramps will get it fixed for you. He's good at things like that."

"His past is very…colorful," I add.

"How colorful?" Iris asks with raised eyebrows.

"He's been to prison," Tate tells her. "But that was a while ago. It seems like he finally has his shit together."

"Wow," Iris whispers. "That's scary."

"He's not dangerous. He's not Malakai. He just took some stupid risks, looking to make a quick buck," I explain.

"I'm glad he's not dangerous," Iris says.

"He's too old to be a real threat, even if he were still in the life," Tate says.

"You going to say that to his face?" I ask my sister, knowing she'd never have the guts to actually tell my grandfather he was too old for anything.

"Um, no. I'm not stupid."

"Sissy," I say with a smirk aimed at my sister.

"I don't want to hurt his feelings."

"Oh yeah, because you care about people's feelings," I tell her, remembering all the times she's stomped on people's feelings with her big black leather boots.

Tate lifts a shoulder. "Sometimes I care, sometimes I don't. Anyway, I think I picked out a few cute things that will fit you perfect," she says to Iris, changing the subject. "My grandparents won't care. They understand the situation."

"I don't think I understand the situation," Iris says with a pained smile.

"It'll be over soon," I tell her. "I promise."

Her smile softens, looking more like her real smile. "I believe you," she says as she slips off the stool and grabs the bag Tate brought. "I'm going to try on some of the clothes."

"We'll be here," Tate tells her. "I'll stay in case none of it works and I have to make a trip to the store."

"I don't want to be a bigger problem than I already am."

"You're not a problem. Go," Tate says, lifting her chin toward the bedroom. "I'm waiting for a fashion show."

"Great," Iris mutters as she stalks toward my bedroom, struggling with the giant bag of clothes, but

I do my best not to run to help her. She already feels helpless in this situation, and the last thing I want to do is make that feeling worse.

As soon as the bedroom door closes, Tate turns her stare on me. "What in the actual fuck?"

"I know. I know. It's crazy," I tell her, keeping my voice quiet so Iris doesn't hear.

"Malakai is a nutjob."

"Yep."

"He's so dangerous."

"I know," I tell her.

Tate scrubs her hands against her face. "She's lucky she's still alive."

I nod.

"If she'd never met you and Gramps didn't know him, she might not still be breathing."

"Fate," I whisper.

Tate sighs. "That's some messed-up destiny."

I shrug.

"What if Malakai won't leave her out of it?"

My stomach turns at the thought. "Impossible."

Tate stares at me without any emotion on her face. "For real?"

"He'll understand."

"For your sake and hers, I hope you're right. I can't believe her ex, who I knew was an asshole for leaving her at the altar, but this goes beyond anything horrible I thought about him. How stupid is he?"

"Dumber than we could've ever imagined. Iris is

beside herself." I dump the remaining coffee in my mug down the drain and place the cup in the sink.

Tate moves around the island to stand next to me. "If anyone can keep her safe, it's you, baby brother. I can tell you're worried, even if you won't say it."

I turn, resting my hip against the counter. "I know Malakai. I know he can be an asshole, but I refuse to believe he won't listen to common sense about her relationship to Lucas. If he doesn't, I'll put myself between her and anything his men will throw at her."

Tate's face pales. "You really like her, huh?"

"I do," I tell her, refusing to lie about my feelings. "Something different about her."

"Aw, my brother's in love."

"It's too early for that."

"I told you, you're marrying her."

I roll my eyes. "Stop, Tate."

The bedroom door opens, and we turn our heads toward the other side of the loft. Iris steps out, wearing a black sweater and skintight jeans.

"You wear that better than me," Tate tells her.

I'm too busy gawking at the fit of the clothes and the outline of her body that they show.

"You don't think it's too tight?" Iris says, pulling a bit at the sweater.

"It's perfect," I tell her, my voice a little hoarse from the need that overwhelms me.

"If you say so," Iris says softly.

"You'll fit right in," Tate adds.

"Is this the outfit I'm going to die in?" Iris peers up at us, her eyes shining less brightly than they usually do.

Tate hops off the stool and heads toward Iris, grabbing her hands as soon as she's close enough. "Babe, look at me." She waits a moment for Iris to gather herself. "You're not dying today unless the universe has it out for you. I have faith in my gramps, and you should too."

Iris stares at Tate with a slight quiver to her bottom lip. "Okay," she whispers as Tate squeezes her hand.

I stalk across the loft, making quick work of the distance, until I'm next to them. "In a few hours, this will all be a memory," I say, wrapping my hand around her upper arm and hauling her to my chest. "I promise it's almost over."

Iris curls her fingers around the material of my T-shirt as she nuzzles against my chest, placing the top of her head under my chin. "I believe you."

Tate looks up at me, her eyes saying everything without moving her lips.

I'm a goner for Iris, and no matter how much I want to deny it, Tate may be right.

Iris just might be the one.

CHAPTER 12
IRIS

BEFORE TODAY, I'd never been around a group of strangers who felt more like family than my own blood.

"Iris, honey. Do you want another serving?" Brax's grandma, Betty, asks me as she stands over me with a spatula full of eggplant parm. But it's not just regular eggplant parm. It's the best I've ever tasted… exactly as promised.

"Um." I glance down at my empty plate, wondering if I'll even be able to walk after this meal.

"You have room for a little more," she says, not waiting for me to say yes before sliding the mountain of cheese-covered veg onto my plate.

Tate laughs at my side. "You have to learn to say no to her or else you'll need a new wardrobe."

I drag my eyes to hers, already wishing I had on a

pair of leggings with an elastic waist instead of her skintight jeans. "I can't say no. Not yet."

Gigi, the cousin from Florida, rubs her stomach. "Your parm may be better than my grams'," she says to Betty.

Betty stops dead in her tracks and turns toward Gigi with the biggest smile on your face. "That's quite a compliment."

I lean over toward Tate, dropping my voice. "I don't know what you two were talking about. Your grandmother is lovely."

Tate stares at me without a smile. "Wait until after dinner. She's being good right now."

My stomach turns, and I'm not sure if it's because of what happens after the meal is served or because I ate enough to feed a small family of people and not just myself. "Great," I whisper.

"I love nights like this," Brax's grandfather—Tino, as he told me to call him—says from the head of the table.

He's exactly how I pictured him after hearing his voice over the phone while he talked to Brax. He's stunningly handsome with his salt-and-pepper hair. I can imagine the way he had the ladies swooning in his younger years because I'm pretty sure, even at his age, he could be quite the catch for women even decades younger than himself.

Will Brax look like him in forty years? Probably. There isn't an ordinary-looking person around this table. Not even the ones who married into the family. I suddenly feel plain in a world of pretty, and that doesn't often happen to me.

I'm not stunning or model-worthy. I'm cute with thick curves, big boobs, and a nose that I'm thankful I'll never need to have surgery on to have it fit my face. I'm not conceited about my looks, nor am I down on myself either. I'm happy with who I am, how I look, and how my body fills out a pair of jeans…even if they're too tight tonight.

Tate and Gigi look like they could be sisters. The genes are strong in this family even when passed down along different familial lines. Gigi's grandfather and Tate's grandfather are brothers, and it shows. But it's their husbands who have caught my attention even more. They're both brooding men, covered in tattoos and facial hair that would make most every woman drool with a single glance. It's like they ordered them out of a catalogue of pure male, inked perfection.

And as my gaze swings to Brax, I realize he'd be on a page in that same catalogue. Dark hair, dark eyes, covered in tattoos, the right amount of facial hair to deliciously prickle my skin if he nestled between my legs.

"Babe," Tate says, elbowing me. "You okay?"

I blink a few times, clearing my thoughts. "Yeah. Why?"

"I was talking to you, and you zoned out. It's like you went somewhere else."

I don't want to tell her that I was thinking about how hot her man is, because hot damn…he is.

"I'm in an eggplant coma."

She gives me a big smile. "Been there. Done that. Sometimes I take a trip there, but I try not to overeat. All the cheese goes right to my hips."

Wylder slides his arm around his wife's chair, leaning into her space until his mouth is next to her ear. "I love those hips. They were made for me."

Tate's face pinkens as she turns her face toward him until their lips are almost touching. "Not here," she whispers.

I swallow, suddenly burning from the inside. He oozes alpha male sexuality with a heavy dose of virility.

Wylder's eyes search hers. "We have the house to ourselves tonight, and I plan to take full advantage of the time alone and your body."

My breath lodges in my throat. Damn. If she's not panting yet, I know she will be soon. I'm panting for the both of us, and I'm not even the one he's talking to.

"Save room for dessert!" Betty yells from the kitchen.

"Shit. I don't know if I can eat anything else," Gigi says softly so Betty can't hear.

Pike, Gigi's husband, covers her hand with his. "You're lucky I don't feel the same way." He winks at her, and I almost fall off my chair.

Betty walks into the room with a giant casserole dish and stops near her husband. Santino wraps his arm around her legs, gripping her thigh. "Whatcha got, baby?"

Betty gazes down at him, and I can see the love in her eyes and his too. "Your favorite."

"Tiramisu?" he asks her, trying to peek into the dish.

"That's your favorite dessert, isn't it?" she asks him, showing him the most beautiful tiramisu I've ever seen.

"Besides you, it is," he replies.

I fan myself with my fingers. The sexual energy from everyone is overwhelming.

"Old people," Tate mutters. "Ick."

"You okay?" Brax asks me this time, sliding his hand onto my thigh before giving me a squeeze.

I close my eyes, trying to block out the urge to throw myself at him in front of everyone. "Just hot," I tell him.

"You want to step outside and cool off?" he asks, sliding his chair out.

"Please," I tell him. "Just for a minute."

As soon as his hand moves from my thigh, I instantly miss the contact and the heat. "Come on," he says, holding out his hand to me.

I slide my palm against his, and I ignore the way my body reacts from the contact. It's like his grandmother put an aphrodisiac into the food tonight. What in the world is wrong with me?

"Don't go for long. Coffee's almost ready," Betty says as she glances our way.

"Five minutes, Gram," he replies as he pulls me up from my chair like I weigh nothing.

Betty smiles with a dip of her head. "I'll dish you out two plates. Iris, do you want me to wrap up your eggplant to go?"

"I'd love that," I tell her, hoping I'll still be breathing when tomorrow comes so I can enjoy the leftovers.

"You got it, sweetheart," Betty says with a wink.

Brax pulls me gently toward the stairs that go down into the bar. His grandparents live above the space and have since they opened the bar decades ago. I have no idea what it's like being in the same spot for so long. I moved around enough in my life that I'm not sure where home is sometimes.

As soon as the cold air of the alley hits my skin, I'm able to take my first deep breath in hours.

"Hey," Brax says, pulling me toward him until my body is flush with his.

I tip my head back, staring up into his dark eyes in the dim lighting outside the bar. "Hey," I whisper as my gaze dips to his mouth.

"You good?"

"I'm better," I breathe, pressing my chest into his.

He places his palm against my cheek, brushing his

thumb underneath the curve of my bottom lip. "Is this okay?"

"Yes," I whisper as my entire body tingles from the contact with his body.

He bends his neck, bringing his lips close to mine as his eyes are glued to me. "Still okay?"

"Yes," I say, my voice cracking as my body buzzes with anticipation.

Yeah, Betty definitely put something in that eggplant. If everybody in their apartment feels like I do, there're going to be a few babies arriving before this time next year.

The cool air crackles around us like it's charged with some invisible sexual force.

"I've been dying to do this all day," he says softly.

I've been dying for him to do it too. I wondered if he'd changed his mind about getting involved with me because of all the crap with Lucas and Malakai. Ever since we got out of bed, things seemed to shift, but I guess I'm wrong. This moment proves that nothing has changed. Brax wants me as much as I want him.

"Do it," I tell him, curling my fingers into the soft material at the back of his hoodie.

His mouth touches mine as I squeeze my eyes shut, watching the fireworks behind my eyelids. The kiss isn't soft. Brax takes what he wants, and I give it to him willingly, losing myself in him.

I kiss him back like it's the last time, and it might be. If things go bad with Malakai tonight... I push that thought from my head, refusing to think about anything except this moment and this kiss.

Brax digs his fingers into the skin at the back of my neck, sending tingles scattering everywhere in my body. I wanted him before, but now the yearning is so overwhelming, I'm not sure I could stay upright without an arm around my back.

If I could drop to my knees right now and worship him, I would. But I remind myself we're in public. Anyone could see. Tonight isn't about that either. Not even this moment is about that. This is about the connection we feel and the need to connect in a way we couldn't in front of his family.

Our tongues tangle as our breathing grows more rushed. "I want you," I moan into his mouth, done hiding exactly how I feel.

I've wasted enough of my life the last few years, thinking there had to be something wrong with me for Lucas to ditch me at the last moment. I picked poorly, and I'm not going to do that again. If Brax is anything like the men in that apartment upstairs, he'll worship me the same way those men worship their wives. I want that. I need that. I could have that with Brax. My heart knows that. My body knows that. And now my mind does too.

The sound of wood scraping in the distance hits my ears but does nothing to make me stop as I move my fingers under his hoodie, finding the hot skin of his lower back.

"Coffee's ready." His grandmother's voice fills the alley.

Brax breaks the kiss and hisses. "Sorry," he says as he rests his forehead against mine, trying to drag in a deep breath.

I feel dizzy and drunk, but not because of the small amount of wine I had with dinner. This is the effect Brax has on me. My entire world spins out of control when our bodies connect. It's as if all the stars in the darkened sky above us aligned and a cosmic event happened when we joined together to form one entity.

"It's okay," I tell him, seeing Betty watching us from the window above the bar.

"We'll finish this later," Brax says before he straightens his body and pulls his forehead away from mine. "And that's a promise."

My knees somehow get weaker at the promise of things to come, and Brax tightens his arm around me as if he knows the effect his words will have on me.

"You're going to be my dessert."

I can only stare up at him. The need that fills me is too much to allow me the ability to form any coherent words.

"It's getting cold," Betty says, not giving us any more time alone.

"Tiramisu is cold," Brax calls out to her.

"The coffee," she says back.

"You ready for this?" he asks.

"I'm ready for anything," I tell him, but I leave out the part about being able to face anything as long as he's with me. I've never felt the type of safety I feel when he's near me, and it's almost unnerving the power he has over me.

"Here we go," he says as he takes my hand and heads toward the back door.

Somehow, I polish off the plate of tiramisu and the entire cup of coffee. I think a part of me figured as long as there was something in my mouth, I wouldn't think about being dessert later or having to answer any questions.

I am wrong on both counts.

"How did you two meet?" his grandmother asks.

"She was at the bar," Brax tells her, his hand covering mine, stroking his thumb across my skin.

"A drinker, eh?" Betty asks as she eyes me.

I shake my head. "No. I can't."

"You can't?" she asks, the confusion clearly written all over her face.

"A medical condition. I can have a drink, but anything more is a problem."

"No. She was there to meet someone," Brax tells her, skating right over the issue with me sleepwalking when I have a little too much, especially if it is hard liquor.

"A friend?" Betty asks again.

"Blind date, but they didn't show," I say with a shrug. Thank God they didn't too, or I wouldn't be here right now. I very well could've been dead at this point because of Lucas.

"Their loss is my gain," Brax tells his grandmother.

"And the weather was shit, so she stayed in the apartment above Inked," Tate tells her grandmother. "And he stayed too."

A smile forms on Betty's lips. "And this man...the one who got you into trouble with Malakai?"

Brax squeezes my hand and thankfully speaks before I have a chance to. "He's her ex from years ago."

"Men," Betty mutters. "Always a pain in the ass."

No truer words.

Betty continues, "Well, it's perfect timing that you found my grandson when you did. It's like you two were put together for a reason. Malakai isn't a man to mess with, but luckily for you, Tino and he have a relationship."

"The world works in mysterious ways," I say to her, peering over at Brax, who's staring back at me.

"At least it's your ex," Gigi says, wading into conversation. She tips her head toward her husband. "This one pulled me into some shit in his personal life that almost left me dead."

"Hey," Pike says as he strokes the top of her shoulder with his fingers. "I had no idea my dad was into bad shit."

"He wasn't just into bad shit—he almost killed me with his bare hands," she argues.

My eyes widen in shock.

"I saved you, darlin'. I'd never let anyone hurt you, not even my father," he says to her before brushing his lips against her temple.

"We've all been traumatized by the men in our lives," Betty says with a sigh. "Tino brought more shit into our lives than I care to remember or can even explain in detail…"

"Wylder never traumatized me," Tate replies to Betty before she can finish her statement.

"The ex-wife," Betty says with a pointed glare.

Wylder lifts a hand and dips his chin. "I can't control that crazy-ass woman."

"Is she still a problem?" Betty asks him and not her granddaughter.

"She's been dealt with and is no longer an issue."

I want to ask what that means because it sounds more sinister than it probably is—at least, I hope so.

"She's completely out of the picture." Tate smiles at her grandmother. "For good."

Tino's chair scrapes against the hardwood as he pushes it back. "I'm going to steal Brax and Iris to talk about what's going to happen tonight," he announces to the table.

"Be quick," Betty tells him.

"Woman, it'll take as long as it takes," he says as he swats her ass playfully, earning himself a glare that's so intense it would make me wither. "Ten minutes, tops."

"Fine," she says.

Brax rises and I follow, leaving the warm company of the dining room to figure out how we're going to get rid of Malakai and keep me breathing.

I'm not ready to die.

I want more of whatever tonight was for as long as I can possibly have it.

CHAPTER 13
BRAX

THE IRISH PUB is more crowded than I expected. I figured since it was a notorious criminal's favorite spot, it would be a little more desolate.

Iris is clutching my hand tightly like she might float away if she loosens her grip. "We're okay," she says to herself, repeating the phrase for the tenth time since we climbed out of my truck.

My gramps gives us an easy smile over his shoulder as we follow him and one of Malakai's lackeys through the mass of people and chairs.

"We're okay," she says again with big eyes, and she's breathing so hard, I worry she's going to faint.

"Hey," I squeeze her hand, breaking the cycle she's been in for the last few minutes. "I promise it's almost over. I won't let anything happen to you."

Iris nods, but the look of panic doesn't leave her

face. "Okay," she mouths, her voice too soft to hear over the chatter around us.

My grandfather moves through the space with ease, wearing one of his best suits. When he strolled out of his bedroom in the outfit, he said, "A man doesn't go to talk to someone like Malakai about life and death dressed like a bum."

I wasn't about to argue with him. He has more experience in this world than I do, especially with men like Malakai.

As we move deeper into the bar, I use my hand to instinctively place Iris behind me, shielding her from any unforeseen issue.

My gaze darts around the space in front of us, hyperaware of the possible threats. There are too many for me to have any real ability to control the situation.

Malakai rises from behind a table with a giant smile as his eyes land on my grandfather. "Tino," he says in a cheerful tone that totally throws me off-kilter. "It's good to see you, old man."

My grandfather extends his hand to him and laughs. "You're not looking so young yourself anymore either, Kai."

Malakai shakes my grandfather's hand, and it feels more like a reunion of old friends than a matter of life and death. "Sit. Sit," Malakai tells him as the handshake ends.

"You remember my grandson," my grandpa says as he glances over his shoulder to where I'm standing.

Malakai's gaze lands on me, and he pauses halfway in the sitting position as if stuck. "That can't be Brax. I remember when he was a wee lad."

"Brax has never been wee," Gramps tells Malakai as he eases into an open chair across from the mobster.

"I suppose not," Malakai says, finally planting his ass back in his chair.

"And his girlfriend, Iris," Grandpa adds as we move closer to the table.

I pull out a chair for Iris, and she gives me a terrified smile before she sits. "Thanks," she says as her voice quavers.

"Malakai," I say, greeting him as I take a seat between my grandfather and Iris.

"Hey, kiddo," Malakai says, sounding every bit like my grandfather with the nicknames. "Time moves quickly, eh?"

"Too fast," Gramps says as he reaches for an empty glass and the pitcher of dark beer in front of him. "Thank you for taking this meeting."

Malakai strokes his reddish-blond beard. "Of course. I was confused at first. I'd never heard Iris's name before you called."

Great.

If she wasn't on his radar, we put her there.

I slide my hand onto Iris's leg, closing my fingers

around the top to ground her, hopefully calming a bit of the energy that's practically vibrating off her.

"But Lucas… Him, I know too well," he adds with a sinister smile, showing the slight gap in his front teeth. "He owes me more than he can probably ever earn in his lifetime."

My grandfather pours the beer with ease, not a single tremor in his hands, as if we're discussing old memories and not the immediate threat. "Iris hasn't dated him in years, but the boy called her to warn her you're coming after her."

Malakai laughs and shakes his head. "Tino, come on. You've known me for what…fifty years? Have I ever gone after women or children?"

My grandfather slides the pitcher of beer toward me as if I'm in the mood to have a drink right now. "No. I can't say I remember a time when that was ever your MO."

"The beef is between Lucas and me, not the girl."

Iris's tense leg muscles relax a little under my palm, and I wonder if Malakai's toying with us.

"So, I have your word that no harm will come to her?" Gramps asks as he lifts the glass of beer to his lips.

Malakai holds up a hand. "No harm will come to her from my hands."

My grandfather places the beer back on the table, but he keeps his eyes trained on Malakai. "And the hands of any man in your organization," my gramps adds, lifting a brow.

I stare at my grandfather in utter surprise. I wouldn't have thought to ask for the clarification. I would've accepted Malakai's word at face value because I didn't grow up in this world of double-talk, backroom deals, and illegal activity.

"I have no beef with her. She wasn't on my radar before you called, and she isn't on it now. Lucas is the only person who will pay for what he owes me, Tino. I won't let anyone, including my men and myself, touch the girl. You have my word as men and old friends."

My grandfather lifts his glass, raising it over the table. "I'm going to hold you to it. Or else…"

Malakai lifts his glass too. "There's no or else. Nothing will happen. My word is my bond."

Iris leans over and whispers, "I feel like I'm in an old gangster movie."

I turn my gaze toward her, trying my best to hold in my laughter, which doesn't seem right in this situation. "Same."

"So, I'm okay? It's done?" she asks, her hair spilling over my arm as she looks across the table at Malakai.

"It's done," I tell her, squeezing her leg again. "Lucas lied."

Malakai wasn't going to come after Iris, and Lucas knew that. Whether he was just trying to get back in her life romantically or looking to score some money off her to keep Malakai off his back, I'm not sure yet. It might've been a combination of both.

"I'll kill him myself," she hisses as she straightens up in her chair.

"I'd help, but I think Malakai will handle it for us," I say to her as I reach for the pitcher of beer.

"I almost feel bad for Lucas. Almost," she says.

"Men like him don't need your pity," I reply.

Iris clears her throat before saying, "Can I ask something?"

Malakai's green eyes move toward Iris, finally focusing on her for the first time since we sat down.

"May I ask what he borrowed the money for?"

Malakai shrugs. "I don't ask questions, darlin'. They ask, I loan."

"Well, that doesn't seem like a good business practice," she says casually, as if she isn't talking to the head of the most powerful Irish crime family in all of Chicago.

I stop breathing as soon as the words leave her mouth. This could go bad in a heartbeat. Malakai doesn't seem like a man who has a sense of humor, even though he's had a smile on his face almost the entire time we've been there.

But to my surprise, Malakai's lips curve up before he lets out the loudest laugh I may have ever heard. "It probably isn't, but it's served me well over the years. I like you," he says, waving a finger at Iris. "I like a woman who speaks her mind."

When I glance at Iris, she's white as a ghost, even though she's smiling back at him. I don't think she meant to say those words out loud, but she did, nonetheless. "I'm sorry," she says quickly, realizing her error but ignoring his reply.

"What do you do, Iris?" Malakai asks, which is something I haven't bothered to do yet.

"I'm a painter," she says.

"Like a house painter?" he shoots back.

I stare at her. I can't imagine her in overalls covered in paint from head to toe. I mean, women do all sorts of things now, but I can't wrap my mind around her on a crew of painters.

She shakes her head. "Canvas."

"An artist," he whispers. "I love it. Oil?"

"Mixed media."

His eyebrows rise in surprise like he has a clue what she's talking about. I sure as hell don't. Mixed media sounds like something I'd watch on television, not a form of art.

"Impressive."

"What's that?" I ask, sounding as stupid as I clearly am when it comes to the art world.

"I use different things," she explains, and I know she's dumbing it down for me because "things" isn't an art term I've heard used before, "to create one piece of art. Like, I may use oil paint, along with spackle and foam or really anything I can get my hands on, to create a single piece of art."

I wonder if she creates her artwork half dressed, trying to avoid ruining her clothes. I can picture it in my mind, her hair flowing over her shoulders in a messy ponytail, a long white button-down shirt, and spatters of paint all over the exposed parts of her skin. I shake the image out of my head, clearly having watched one too many unrealistic movies about artists.

"Do you make a living off your work?" Malakai asks, lifting his hand and motioning at someone across the bar.

"I do. I'm very lucky and have a big audience on social media."

I stare at her, completely impressed by her ability to turn her love from a hobby into a career.

"I could use a new piece in this bar. I've been staring at the same big-box-store artwork pieces for the last decade. We need a refresh. Are you game?" Malakai asks her.

A growl escapes my throat, but no one else can hear it over Iris's reply of "Sure."

"We'll talk price another day, but now, we do a shot to conclude our business."

Iris slides her eyes to me, wanting help with the drinking after she just agreed to create pieces for a mobster. It doesn't matter what type of business you agree to. None of it is good when it comes from this lawless world.

"Can you handle one?" I ask her, knowing there will be blowback if we reject the shot. Men like Malakai have ways they like to do things, and any change in their script could throw everything off in an instant.

"One should be okay," she says with a slight shrug of her shoulder. "Maybe I should stay with you tonight so I don't wind up wandering around on the streets."

Suddenly, this is turning into a win-win for me. I wanted her to stay the night. Last night was a bust because we were both in a panic over the possibility of someone coming after her. The night didn't end the way either of us had planned. But this gives me an opening to make what should've happened last night become reality.

"That's a good idea," I tell her.

I could kiss Malakai for making a shot a requirement to end our business.

Four shot glasses filled with amber liquid, which I assume is whiskey, are placed in the middle of the table by a waitress who doesn't bother speaking to anyone. Malakai pushes three of them our way before he grabs the last one for himself.

"A toast," he says, lifting his hand.

My grandpa raises his glass before Iris and I do the same.

Malakai smiles, looking like a normal old man

instead of the criminal we all know he is. "May you be in heaven a full half an hour before the devil knows you're dead."

Iris and I look at each other when my grandfather says, "Cin cin," as he tips his head at Malakai.

"Sláinte," Malakai replies before he brings the glass to his lips and downs the liquid in one gulp.

"Well," I say to Iris, tapping her glass with mine. "To another day."

"Another day," she says, watching me as I swallow the alcohol.

Iris winces, and as soon as she inhales, she starts to cough. "That…was…rough," she barely gets out while she tries to clear her throat as I take the glass from her hand.

I've been in her shoes, choking on a liquor I hadn't quite been prepared for, and it sucks.

"We good?" Gramps asks Malakai.

Malakai gives him a chin lift. "We're good." But before we have a chance to stand, Malakai turns his gaze on Iris. "You want to make a little extra cash?"

"Um," she says as I turn my body toward her, wishing I could telepathically communicate with her.

There isn't a job or favor on this planet Malakai would want her to do that's worth any amount of money he wants to pay her to do.

Her eyes slide to mine, and I do my best to give her the hell-no face, even if we don't know each other well enough for her to be able to read all my facial expressions.

"Um," she mumbles.

"I'll give you fifty thousand if you talk to Lucas and find out where that weasel's hiding."

Fifty thousand is a lot of freaking money, but she has to know, if she does it, it'll be the last place Lucas will ever take a breath of air.

"While I appreciate the offer, I can't. I won't. I refuse to talk to him, even for that sum of money."

She answered politely, but I don't know if I should be concerned that she didn't say it would be wrong because he'd end up dead.

"Mental health reasons," she says before giving Malakai a kind smile.

"Understood," Malakai says through gritted teeth. He's not happy about it, but he can't force her either.

"Shall we?" Gramps asks me. "It's getting late."

"Past your bedtime?" Malakai asks my grandpa.

"Something like that," Gramps says to him.

"I was hoping you'd stay and drink with me."

"Betty would have my balls, Kai, and then she'd come for yours."

Malakai slaps the table and chuckles. "I always liked her."

I feel like there's so much I don't know about my grandparents at this point. I don't think I ever will either. The fact that my grandmother knows Malakai well enough that he's always liked her is intriguing and alarming at the same time. That doesn't even take into account all my grandfather's activity before and after prison. My family has a wild past, but hopefully it all stays buried because my generation doesn't have a damn thing to do with it.

I move first, pushing my chair back and standing before helping Iris from her seat. "Ready?"

"More than ready," she says, locking her eyes with mine as she climbs to her feet. "This was…"

"Yeah." I have no words to fully explain the last handful of minutes, and I'm pretty sure she doesn't either. "Thank you," I say to Malakai as I turn my attention toward him.

"Be well," Malakai replies like we didn't just have a discussion about keeping my girlfriend alive for something her ex-fiancé did.

I slide my arm around Iris's back, ushering her through the bar toward the exit. Iris glances over her shoulder, giving me a tight smile as I hold open the door for her.

"It's all over?" she asks as we step into the frigid night air.

"It is," I say, waiting for my grandpa to join us.

"Thank God," she breathes, lifting her cupped hands to her mouth to keep them from freezing.

Gramps slides a hand over the side of his head, smoothing down his always-perfect hair. "Problem solved," he says, glancing around the street like he always does. It's like he expects the boogeyman to jump out of nowhere, but I guess in his past life, that was a very real possibility.

Iris throws her arms around my grandpa's shoulders, burying her face in the crook of his neck. "Thank you. Thank you. Thank you."

Gramps raises his eyebrows for a second before his face softens, and he wraps his arms around her. "You're welcome, sweetheart. It got the old blood pumping. I forgot how exciting that world can be."

Iris pulls back, blinking at him. "What? That was insane."

Gramps smiles at Iris, not the least bit upset about her comment. "Sometimes you need a little danger to remind yourself you're still alive."

I pull Iris next to me, securing her to my side. "Why don't you go home and tell Grandma that?"

"She's the most dangerous one of all." His smile widens. "It's going to be a good night, kiddo." He slaps my back like he's celebrating.

I do my best not to gag because I know he's talking about what's going to happen when he gets home.

My grandparents do not have sex. My grandparents do not have sex. I repeat the statement to myself as we climb into the car.

"Breathe," Iris says with a laugh in her voice. "We'll be old someday too."

"Not helping," I grumble.

"It may be a good night for you too," she says, low enough that my grandpa doesn't hear her.

And suddenly, anything else I was thinking vanishes, and I can't wait to drop off the old man and get back to my place with my girl.

CHAPTER 14
IRIS

"YOU'VE GOT to be kidding me." Mikayla rubs her temples like I'm giving her a headache. "At what point can we be the ones to stop Lucas from breathing?"

I wave my paintbrush at her and shake my head. "He's in the past. I'm not giving him another thought, and neither should you."

Sandy strolls in, typing away on her phone screen. "Sorry I'm late," she says before looking up at us. "What'd I miss?"

"So much," Mikayla mutters. "Be prepared to feel stabby."

Sandy's eyebrows shoot up toward her hairline. "Shit. That bad?"

"Worse than you can imagine," Mikayla answers.

I keep working on my newest project, ignoring

them and their dramatics. I've had enough in the last few days to last me a lifetime.

Sandy hefts her oversized purse onto the tabletop, throwing her phone inside before she pulls out a bottle of wine. "I brought refreshments," she announces with her lips turned up.

"We're going to need them," Mikayla says, leaning over, propping her elbow on top of the table, and placing her face in the palm of her hand.

"Drama queen," I whisper into the canvas I've been working on for the last hour.

"Almost dying isn't drama," Mikayla shoots back.

Sandy stops mid-twist of the cap to her fancy bottle of wine she loves. "What?" Her voice comes out as a high-pitched screech. "How? Who?"

"You forgot where, why, and when," I say, trying to be funny, but when I slide my gaze to them, I see the joke didn't hit the way I thought it would.

"I can't believe you're joking about this." Mikayla shakes her head and growls. "This isn't a time for funnies."

"It's always a time for funnies," I argue.

"I think we're going to need this too," Sandy says as she pulls out a flask from what seems like a bottomless pit of a purse.

"What the hell else do you have in there?" I ask her, hoping we'll talk about something else besides the last two days of my life.

"Oh no, you're not," Sandy says, wagging a finger at me as she slides onto the stool next to Mikayla. "We're not going to let you derail this conversation."

"I shouldn't have said anything," I mumble and then sigh.

"We tell one another everything," Sandy says as she pulls out three glasses from the same purse.

"Is there anything else in there besides a traveling bar?" I say, staring at the bag like it's magical because there's no other way all that stuff would fit in there.

Sandy shrugs and lifts her hands. "Not really. This is my party purse. It only has one purpose, and it's booze."

"Don't answer her questions until she answers ours," Mikayla tells her.

"Brutal," I whisper, dipping my paintbrush into the black paint to get the tiniest amount.

Sandy pours three glasses of wine, one of them smaller than the others, which is for me. "Now, talk," she says as she pushes the wine across the table to Mikayla and me.

"I don't think you're prepared," Mikayla tells her.

"I will be after this," Sandy says before she lifts the glass to her lips and downs the wine like it's a shot.

I stare at her in disbelief. "Jesus."

"He's not here, but we are. Confess." Mikayla gives me a pointed glare. "Now."

I sigh, leaving the wine where Sandy put it. I

spend the next ten minutes telling the entire story again to Sandy, while Mikayla gives additional commentary like she's a background narrator in my story.

"Jeez," Sandy says when I finally stop talking.

"Jeez?" Mikayla asks Sandy with big eyes. "That's all you got?"

Sandy lifts her chin. "I'm still processing."

"But I'm fine. It's over."

"You almost were over," Mikayla adds.

"I want to murder Lucas," Sandy says, rubbing her hands together like her brain is working on a plan.

"I think Malakai has that covered," Mikayla replies.

She isn't wrong. I doubt a man like Malakai is going to let Lucas skate on his debt without paying some price, and I assume it will be his life.

"How weird is it that Brax's family knows him?" Sandy asks, but she isn't being mean. I can see the innocence in her question written all over her face.

"I haven't lost sight of that fact either. My family doesn't know any mobsters. Does yours, Sandy?" Mikayla asks.

Sandy shakes her head.

"I was all for team Braxasaurus-Rex, but now…" Mikayla's lips turn down as she pulls in a long, deep breath, "Now, he's slipping in my rankings of dream man for you."

"Oh, stop," I say, laughing that she used the

same nickname for him as I did because I never uttered it to another soul. I'm certain we aren't the first people to think of it either, but our minds do work the same, which isn't shocking since we're best friends.

"Brax isn't part of that world. His grandfather knew him from the neighborhood. His family has owned that bar for decades. I'm sure they know everyone from that area."

Mikayla stares at me, blinking a few times with an otherwise blank face. "Uh-huh," she mumbles.

"His grandfather is a sweet man," I continue, ignoring Mikayla and her skepticism—even if she is right, I'll never admit it. "He totally had my back and cleared everything up."

"Yeah, that's something an old, retired bartender would do. I mean, I'm sure I can call a mobster and have a sit-down with him because I served him a beer thirty years ago." Mikayla rolls her eyes as she lifts the wine to her mouth, finally filling her yapper with something other than words.

"What does it matter?" Sandy asks Mikayla as she refills her wineglass again. "She's safe now. I don't care who knows who as long as no one is coming after her because Lucas is a giant douchebag."

I haven't touched my wine yet, but these two are guzzling theirs down like it's an Olympic sport. Sometimes I wish I didn't sleepwalk and talk. I want to be normal, but then I think of all the times I've seen them with hangovers and massive headaches, and I count myself a little lucky.

"Are you sure Brax is clean?"

"Clean?" I ask, playing stupid.

"He's not, you know…" She presses her nose to the side. "Crooked."

"He's clean," I promise her. "If, and it's a big if, his grandpa was into anything bad, Brax is not. He's a normal guy."

Sandy snorts. "Is there such a thing as a normal guy? I haven't met one yet."

Mikayla and I giggle because she isn't far off base, but Brax is the closest to normal I've met.

"I met some of his family."

Their laughter dies in an instant.

"You did?" Mikayla asks with wide eyes.

"When?" Sandy adds, jerking her chin back like the news is so shocking, she's about to fall over.

"Before the meeting with the bad guy." I don't bother looking at them. I know Mikayla's wheels are already spinning in that alcohol-soaked brain.

"Who?" Sandy asks.

"His grandma, his sister—but I'd already met her —her man, and two cousins from Florida."

"Wow, you're moving fast, like a high-speed train heading straight toward a cliff where the tracks end," Mikayla says.

"It was nice."

"Nice?" Sandy's voice lifts higher than usual. "Meeting someone's family is never nice."

It's my turn to roll my eyes. "His was. His grandma is a great cook. And his sister and cousins were funny. They're an interesting family."

"I'm sure," Mikayla mutters.

"Hey." I point my paintbrush at her. "I met him because of your bright idea to put me on a dating app against my will. Now that things are working out and I'm putting myself out there, you're all filled with snark. Either be happy for me or zip it."

Mikayla stares at me, her eyebrows up and her mouth tight. "You're right," she says.

That statement had to feel like a dagger going straight into her heart. There's no one who likes to admit they're wrong less than Mikayla.

"Wow. You did drink a lot. Maybe you should stop," Sandy says, knowing Mikayla as well as I do.

"I'm still sober," Mikayla says, giving Sandy the side-eye. "But that's only because you're being greedy and drinking it all yourself."

"Whatever," Sandy says, pushing the wine bottle toward Mikayla with the backs of her fingers. "Fill'er up."

"Did you sleep with him yet?" Mikayla asks, helping herself to the small amount that's left in the bottle.

"We slept."

"And what about?" Sandy makes an obscene gesture. "You know…"

"Not yet."

Mikayla's hand stops midair before she can set the wine bottle back on the table. "You haven't done it yet?"

I shake my head. "We've done other things."

"Dumb," Mikayla mutters.

"We're taking it slow."

"Yeah, 'cause riding him in his truck was super slow," Sandy says, but she doesn't look me in the eyes when she speaks.

"I wasn't myself."

"Uh-huh," Sandy mutters.

"I had planned to sleep with him the night Lucas called."

"God, he's a cockblock. The man has always had the worst timing, and his streak continues," Mikayla says before she goes back to sipping her wine.

"You going to drink that?" Sandy points at my glass.

I shake my head. "He ruined everything that night."

"Well, lucky for you, you're still alive and can still make it happen," Sandy says as she reaches for my little bit of undrunk wine. "You could really use it."

"I've been well taken care of."

Their eyes slide to me.

"Do tell," Mikayla says with a smirk.

"We want all the details. Please tell me his, you know, is bigger than Lucas's," Sandy adds.

"His you know?" Mikayla says into her wineglass. "Are you thirteen?"

Sandy gives Mikayla the middle finger. "Well?"

"Def not like Lucas, and that's all I'm going to say about it."

"Straight or crooked?" Mikayla asks.

I stare at her in shock. "Crooked?"

She nods. "They're not all like spears."

"I'm…well…uh," I stutter, at a complete loss.

"Those bent ones can be a hoot," Sandy says, crooking her pointer finger. "It just hits all the spots."

Mikayla bumps Sandy's shoulder with her own. "Same. I love a little hook."

I have no idea what they're talking about, but that's not surprising. I was in a long-term relationship for most of my adult life while they were busy exploring their sexuality with as many men as they could. I've clearly missed out on the hook, based on their conversation, because besides being small, Lucas's penis was also straight like a small hot dog.

"I thought you two did stuff." Mikayla lifts her hands and bunches her eyebrows together. "What the heck is stuff?"

I shrug. "Stuff."

Sandy spins her stool top around like we used to do in middle school, almost making me dizzy. "Her stuff is kissing."

"You felt it when you rode that jean-clad cock in his truck. You should be able to at least tell the size."

"More than enough," I tell her, trying to keep it simple.

Mikayla just stares at me, her lips pursing in annoyance. "Have you at least seen him shirtless?"

I nod. "Better than I could've imagined."

Mikayla sighs as she reaches over, stopping Sandy's movement, but she keeps her gaze trained on me. "I won't even ask about his pants because if you can't tell me anything about his cock, you haven't seen it even from a distance."

I busy myself in my work again, not wanting to talk anymore about Brax's body and my lack of knowledge about every little inch of it. I plan to rectify the situation, begging if I have to, because I am done with my self-imposed dry streak. I chickened out last night, but I won't make that mistake twice.

"I'm proud of you," Mikayla says, catching me completely off guard.

I lift my gaze to her, thinking she wasn't talking to me, but she was. "For?"

"Putting yourself out there again. We forced your hand, but you hopped on and literally rode it."

Sandy snorts, covering her mouth quickly to hide the noise.

"I hate you both," I mutter.

Mikayla chuckles. "You love us more than anyone else in the world."

"Hardly," I lie. "You're like fifth or sixth on the list."

"Then I know I'm third or fourth. I must be higher than you," Sandy teases Mikayla. "I'm the nicer one."

"When are you seeing him again?" Mikayla asks, ignoring Sandy again.

"Tonight," I tell her. "I'm staying at his place again because his family is having a dinner. It's something they do every week."

"Oh my God," Sandy says, practically squealing with excitement.

"Well, at least you already met them," Mikayla says.

I shake my head, my stomach already turning at how wrong she is. "No. That was only a few people. This is everyone."

Sandy's eyes go wider somehow, and Mikayla claps, showing almost as much excitement as Sandy about the situation.

"Perfect," Mikayla says. "Big step."

I'm not sure I'm ready for a bigger step than I've already taken, but I don't have a choice in it now. I am going to put on my big-girl panties and dive right into the madness. This is what people do when they are in relationships. I am in a relationship. I have reminded myself of that fact multiple times today because it still feels so surreal.

"But the distance is going to be a problem," Mikayla adds.

"It's the same city," I tell her.

"With the worst traffic," she replies.

"We'll figure it out. It's not like I have an office job I have to be at early."

"I see lots of sleepovers in your future," she says.

I smile because, if things go right, I see them too, and they're divine.

CHAPTER 15
BRAX

"THIS IS MY LITTLE BROTHER, MASON," I tell Iris as Mason stands in front of us, staring at her like he's in a trance.

"Hi," Iris says, giving him a smile.

"Hi," Mason says back, still staring.

"You okay?" I ask him because it's not like my little brother to be so limited in his ability to communicate. He's also never this quiet.

He nods slowly. "She's just so…"

Iris gazes at me, worry etched all over her face. I shrug back because I'm at a complete loss as to where he's going, but it sure as hell better not be anywhere bad. If he hurts her feelings, I'll choke him out in front of the entire family.

"So what?" I ask, curling the fingers on my right hand into a fist.

"Pretty," he whispers.

My shoulders relax. "You're an idiot," I mutter.

"You're sweet," Iris says, eating up the compliment.

"Not really," Mason tells her as his lips finally curve upward. "If you ever dump this idiot, I'm single. I'll be a way better boyfriend than he ever could be."

Iris giggles at his stupidity.

"You're testing my patience tonight," I warn him, but in reality, it's not just tonight. He's tested my patience since the day he was born, and I figure he will until my cold body is placed six feet under.

Mason playfully smacks my shoulder. "Keepin' you on your toes, big bro."

"What's going on?" Tate asks as she glances between Mason and me.

"Your brother's being a moron," I tell her.

"You or him?" she asks, earning a glare from me.

"Iris," Tate says, taking Iris by the arm. "I want to introduce you to the girls."

Iris looks at me, and I give her a chin lift. "Do whatever, sweetheart. Everyone's excited to meet you."

"Yeah," Mason mumbles. "I know I was, and man, it was worth the wait." He coughs as I turn my hardened stare at him.

"Lulu and Zoey have been dying to talk to you. You're quite the topic of conversation tonight," Tate tells her as they walk away.

Iris glances over her shoulder to find my eyes, and I smile, wanting her to know she's safe with the other girls. No one in my family is mean, and every single person gets overly excited when there's a new face in the crowd.

"Hey, dipshit. Stop looking at her like that. She's too old for you, and she's mine."

"She's yours?" my brother asks with raised eyebrows.

"Yes," I snarl.

He tilts his head, those damn bushy black eyebrows still raised. "Interesting."

"What the hell is interesting?"

"Never heard you say that about anyone before. I think Tate was right."

"You two gossip like two little old ladies."

"And you've never brought anyone to family dinner. Tate didn't have to say anything to me about Iris to know what's up."

When I swing my gaze in Iris's direction, I see the girls are in a huddle, deep in conversation. "What do you think they're talking about?" I ask my brother, forgetting he's a dumbass when it comes to women.

"You."

Damn. I think he's right for once. When all eyes in the group shift to me, there's no mistaking who the target of their discussion is. Iris gives me a wink from across the room, settling what little bit of anxiety was starting to rise deep inside me.

"See," Mason says, slapping me on the shoulder, "told you."

Dad's not far away from them, and when my eyes lock with his, I know I'm in for a very long conversation. He crosses the room in a few large strides like a man determined.

My dad is a calm guy. He had been through more than most people by the time he hit forty, and somehow, he kept his shit together and came out the other side stronger. But every once in a while, that sleek exterior slips when things start to go sideways.

"Braxton," he says as he stops in front of me.

The dreaded full first name.

Without a moment's hesitation, Mason peels away from us without saying a word, leaving me to deal with Dad on my own.

Jerk.

"Hey, Dad," I say, trying to keep the mood light, because I know he wants to go dark.

Dad scrubs his palm against the beard he's been growing for the last few months at Tilly's request. She says she's in her beard era...whatever that means. "When were you going to tell me about Malakai?"

"Well…" I start to say, stalling for time because I haven't thought much about what I'm going to tell him about the situation.

I thought my grandfather would keep his mouth shut about the meeting, but I was delusional to think he wouldn't sing like a canary.

There are no secrets, dummy.

"I had to hear about everything from my mom," he explains before rubbing the bridge of his nose like he's fighting off a headache.

"I didn't want you to worry."

It's my go-to phrase when I've withheld information before. It worked like a charm when I was younger, but the older I get, the less it works on him. But that doesn't mean I don't do the old Hail Mary and sling it out there like there's a shot it'll satisfy him.

"Worry?" he chuckles, but the sound is far from happy. "More like terrified. It's freaking Malakai."

"It's all over, Dad."

He raises an eyebrow as he stares at me, all hint of his sardonic laughter gone. "It's over?"

I nod. "Gramps sorted it."

He squeezes his eyes shut and sighs. "What was the price?"

"No price. Just a misunderstanding," I tell him.

Dad places his hand on my shoulder, squeezing lightly as he pins me with his gaze. "There's always a price, son."

I wonder what goes through his head sometimes. He seems like an optimist, but the man has a wicked pessimistic streak in him, especially when it comes to things I've done.

"The situation has nothing to do with us. She wasn't even on his radar."

"Is that what Malakai said?"

"Yes."

"The man wouldn't know the truth if it hit him square in the face. Watch your back, and if you see anything suspicious, you call me, not the old man."

"Okay," I say, drawing out the word.

"Grow eyes in the back of your head."

"Got it."

"Do you?" he asks, stepping a foot closer and glancing around to see who's watching us or listening.

"I know Malakai. Not like your grandfather, but I know him well enough to understand nothing is ever over with him, especially when a large amount of money is involved."

"Why does it look like you're discussing his bad report card?" Ma asks, saving me from the conversation.

"It's just Dad being Dad," I tell her as he drops his arm from my shoulder.

His facial expression morphs within a second before he turns his gaze on her. "We're good, love. Just talking about man things."

Ma rolls her eyes. "You're a bad liar, Angelo."

He snakes an arm around her waist and pulls her into his side, nuzzling her neck. "We were talking about his new girlfriend."

"I love her," Ma says as Dad peppers her neck with kisses.

He isn't lying but it wasn't a sweet conversation

like his tone alluded to. I rarely witness Dad lying to her, but when he does, if I didn't know him better, I wouldn't be able to tell. I'm not sure if that's concerning or the man's a genius.

"She's great, baby," Ma says to me as she pushes against my father's chest, trying to find a little space.

"I think so too, Ma." I smile at her, hoping someday I'll have the type of relationship with someone that they have…minus the half-truths, of course.

"The girls really like her too," she adds.

The girl huddle hasn't broken up. They are still deep in conversation, but the laughter coming from their circle fills the room, almost drowning out the chatter of everyone else.

Lulu waves her hand, catching my eye. "I'm being summoned," I tell them, happy to be called away from the big talk with my dad.

"Go. Have fun," Ma says.

"Remember what I said," Dad reminds me like I've somehow forgotten his words of warning in the last thirty seconds.

"I won't forget," I tell him with a tight smile before I dip away from them and stalk toward the table with my sister, my cousins, and my girl.

Lulu pulls out the empty chair next to her when I'm a few feet away. I slide into the seat, giving Iris a small kiss on the cheek, earning myself a smile. When

I turn toward my cousin, she's staring at me with a goofy grin. "Thanks," I tell her.

"That looked tense, cuz. Uncle Ang can be a bit…"

"Much," I tell her with a laugh. "He was being that."

"Everything okay?" she asks, searching my face for some clue.

"Perfect," I reply before turning back toward Iris. "Everything okay over here?"

"I love them," she says, looking every bit happy and relaxed around my cousins and sister. "They're so fun."

"That's one way of describing them," I mumble.

"Lulu wants to come help me organize my art studio."

"Don't do it," I warn Iris as I take her hand in mine. "The girl likes to organize way too much."

"Well, I hate it, so she'll be doing me a favor."

"You'll never be able to find your things again."

Iris laughs, looking like she's always been here. She's comfortable around my family, and nothing in the world could make me happier. My family has always been one of the most important things in my life, and I can't imagine being with someone who doesn't love them as much as I do.

"The girls are taking me out one night this week," she says.

"Drinking?"

She nods. "Them, not me."

"Sure," I tease. "They're not going to let you remain sober while they get wasted."

"Well, I'll just have to stay at your place that night so I don't wander the streets of Chicago half naked and end up behind bars."

"I don't mind sleepwalking Iris."

"You don't mind her? She's still me, you know."

"She's much more handsy."

Iris leans forward, bringing her lips close to mine. "If you're good, maybe I'll get handsy later."

"Sweetheart, I'm always good." I smirk, giving her hand a squeeze.

She sucks in a deep breath as her eyes search mine. "I'm hoping you are because I've never wanted you as much as I do now."

"Who is this bold woman?"

She smiles. "Your family is rubbing off on me."

"I don't know if that's a good thing."

"It is," she says before she licks her lips, causing my stomach to flutter in anticipation.

"Earth to Iris and Brax," Zoey says, snapping her fingers and killing any spark that was zipping around us in the air.

"It's gross but kind of nice to see him like this," Lulu says as Iris pulls back, settling into her chair and facing the group.

As if on cue, Wylder, Mason, and Nino grab chairs and wade into the conversation.

"What'd we miss?" Nino asks.

There isn't a single one of us who's like the others, besides looks. The Italian runs deep in this family in appearance and attitude, but we all have a quirk or two that makes us unique.

Lulu has her need for organization. She doesn't know how to relax unless she's tied down and forced to sit still. She's wound so tight sometimes, I worry she's going to spiral herself right off the edge of mental sanity.

Zoey is a free spirit and flits through life like she doesn't have a care in the world. Two sisters could not be more opposite. Sometimes it's hard for me to come to grips that they grew up in the same household. Zoey didn't get the obsessively clean gene that Lulu got from somewhere…probably her father. There's no denying they're sisters, but they have different biological fathers, and that's where the recipe must've swapped a few ingredients.

Nino is an only child, and he acts like it sometimes too. We've made it our mission as his cousins to keep him grounded in reality. Not everyone is going to service his every whim to make him happy like his parents have done his entire life. He's spoiled but not bratty. Any bit of that part of him was beaten out of him as a little kid by our own hands.

Amelia is also an only child, but Uncle Vinnie and Aunt B made sure she didn't turn into a nightmare. She has Aunt B's sweetness, but she's still young, and that could change as the world makes her more jaded. She has a dream of becoming an author like her mother, already working on her third novel, which is impressive for someone barely into her twenties.

My brother Mason is hoping to join my sister's business at Inked. He has dreams of becoming a world-renowned tattoo artist like our cousins in Florida, but I think he's doing it to get women and for the fame, not the love of the art. He's a good guy, although he's led about by his dick at this point in his life. He's a bit too cocky and sometimes he can get on my nerves, but he's solid and good straight down to his core.

My sister Tate is a mouthy little thing. She beat my ass more times than I can count growing up and is probably the reason why I'm not a hellion as an adult. We've been through a lot of shit together, losing our biological mother when we were little. Tate somehow made me her responsibility even though Dad married Tilly before I really have many memories. She's a great pseudo stepmom to Wylder's two girls and is going to be an amazing mother to her own once she finally pops the news to the entire family about her little bun in the oven.

"So, Wylder and I have an announcement," Tate says to the table, clearing her throat like she does when she's nervous.

Thank God. She's finally going to tell people so I don't have to keep this secret. I complain about the family being gossips, but I'm one too. We don't have secrets, and no one judges anyone for the boneheaded shit we all do. We learn from one another's mistakes…for the most part.

All eyes at the table turn toward her and Wylder, and all talking dies.

Tate glances at Wylder and smiles. "You tell them."

Wylder shakes his head, sliding his arm around Tate's back. "No, baby. This is your family—you tell them."

I brace myself for the screams of joy that are going to shoot around this table, liable to make my ears ring like a sudden explosion too close to my head.

"Okay. Okay." She takes a deep breath and holds out her hand. "We're getting married."

My eyebrows shoot up on their own. That wasn't what I was expecting to come out of her mouth. They call each other husband and wife, and I've fallen into that too. I think of them as married because they act like they are, and they are for all intents and purposes.

"Oh my God, when?" Lulu asks, clapping her hands like it's the most exciting news she's ever heard.

My eyes find Wylder, and he gives me a smile. We both know what's up. He's knocked her up, and now he wants to marry her before the baby arrives. It's not like they have to hide their sex life from the family. We all know they're doing it.

"Congrats, sis," I say to her, giving her a lift of my chin.

"Thanks," she says.

"When? When? When?" Lulu asks again. "We need to start planning."

"A few weeks."

Lulu's eyes grow as big as saucers. "A few weeks?" She sounds personally insulted by such a short timeline. "How?"

"We'll do it here at the bar. Just a small family affair." Any longer than a few weeks and she might be showing.

"We have so much to do," Lulu says, panic filling her eyes.

"We?" Zoey says, rolling her eyes at her sister. "It's Tate's wedding."

"But…" Lulu's shoulders drop, and all excitement vanishes.

"You can plan everything," Tate says to Lulu. "I have all the faith in the world you'll make it the best wedding ever at the Hook & Hustle."

"Wow. That's so exciting," Iris says at my side, her thumb grazing the pad near the bottom of my thumb.

Lulu lunges forward, throwing her arms around Tate's shoulders. "I love you, cousin. I'll make it better than you can ever imagine."

Tate stares at me across the table as she hugs Lulu back, knowing I know there's more to the story than just a wedding.

"You're officially going to be family," Nino says to Wylder. "About damn time."

"I don't need a piece of paper to tell me I'm one of you," Wylder says to him.

"Do Mom and Dad know?" Mason asks Tate.

"Wylder talked to Dad before he asked."

"So they *know* know?" I ask her.

"They know we're getting married," she says, her voice lingering on the last word.

Got it. They don't know everything.

Lulu looks at me and then at Tate. "*Know* know what?"

"About the wedding," Tate lies.

Lulu stares at her, trying to read into the conversation. "You're not telling me something."

"You know everything," Tate tells her. "Is two weeks enough time?"

Lulu clutches her chest and gasps. "Two weeks is cutting it close, but…" And just like that, the secret Tate's keeping that Lulu almost figured out is forgotten.

Grandma, Aunt B, Aunt Daphne, Mom, and Aunt Delilah come out of the kitchen, carrying extremely large bowls of everything they've spent hours whipping up.

"Dinner's ready," Gram announces to everyone as she does every week when we have the same meal at the same time. "I made eggplant parm as an extra treat this week." She winks at Iris when she says that.

"She must love you," Zoey says to Iris. "She doesn't make it very often because it's time-consuming. She's trying to keep you around."

"I don't plan on going anywhere," Iris says.

I give her hand a squeeze, because the last thing I want is for her to vanish. Nothing in my life has felt so right and natural. Being with Iris is easy—although the hiccup with Malakai and Lucas wasn't ideal or, hell, normal.

"I think Tate and Wylder want to make an announcement first," Ma says as they set the bowls down on the bar top so we can all grab what we want. There are too many people for it to be a sit-down dinner where we're served. No one has the time or energy with a group this big. It's a buffet of absolute deliciousness.

Grandma gasps. "Is she finally pregnant?"

"No, Ma," Mom says to Gram, and I almost feel guilty when my gram's face falls.

"Damn," she mutters.

"Tate." Ma motions for Tate to stand as soon as her hands are empty.

Wylder's first to climb to his feet before he helps Tate to stand at his side.

"We're getting married in two weeks," Tate says as soon as she's standing next to him.

The room erupts into joyful chatter and congratulations. I'm happy for my sister. She's the happiest I've seen her in our entire lives. She deserves all the good things that are coming her way.

And with all eyes on her and the upcoming wedding, it takes some of the heat off me. No one's going to be paying attention to every little movement between Iris and me. Instead of being under a microscope, we'll fade into the background and get more privacy than I ever could've imagined possible.

"I'm starving," Iris says, eyeing the plate of eggplant parm.

"Me too, but I'm saving room for dessert." I stare at her profile, knowing exactly what I'm having.

She turns her dark-eyed gaze to me. "What is it?"

"You."

CHAPTER 16
IRIS

MY BOOT barely hits the floor before Brax has me pressed against the back of the door to his loft. "I've been dying to do this all day," he says against my lips, his eyes searching mine for the same need I see in his.

"Me too," I tell him, pulling at his coat to get all the layers of clothes off him.

I hate winter. The amount of clothes I need to wear always makes me feel claustrophobic, but never have I hated it more than in this moment.

Brax's hands are fast as his lips find my neck, tasting the tender skin. Goose bumps break out across my flesh, which seems impossible underneath all the heavy clothes, but his mouth is like magic.

I let my head fall back against the door, giving him more access to my neck, but my fingers never stop working at his zippers and buttons. I don't know if I'm getting anywhere because I'm too busy getting lost in the feeling of him touching me and the warmth of his body pressed against mine in areas that have been begging for his touch since the day I met him.

His nose is cold against my skin as his lips move lower once my coat falls away and the deep V of my sweater becomes easily available to him. "Fuck it," he mutters as his lips skate across my flesh.

His mouth vanishes, and my eyes snap open at the loss of his warmth against my skin. "What…" The words die in my throat as he strips off his shirt. I guess I was moving too slow for him. I tried my best, but it's hard for my brain to work when all I can think about is his lips. My hands don't work well without being told what to do. I haven't had sex in so long, it is no longer something I can do without thinking.

I forgot how good the man looks without a shirt. In the dimly lit loft with so much want coursing through my veins, this man is a damn near masterpiece.

I'd never been one to find heavily tattooed men attractive, but on Brax, I want to lick each line until I have them memorized.

Thankfully, Brax doesn't have a belt on tonight. Maybe he planned ahead, knowing this was how the night was going to end. Either way, I am a happy girl when his fingers make quick work of finishing what I began.

When his jeans hit the floor, I almost gasp. Not only is his cock large, which I knew because I've felt him up so many times and rode him in his truck like a couple of teenagers, but it is decorated.

I've never seen a piercing in anyone's cock before. Never in my life did I think it would look like that, and I never thought the very sight would cause my mouth to water and my clit to ache.

"Wow," I say, my voice all deep and full of need. "That's…" I step forward, reaching out my hand because when I see something spectacular, I always want to touch it. I gaze up at him, unsure of proper protocol when confronted with something like this.

"You can touch it. That's the point of being naked, Iris."

I smile, rolling my eyes internally because, duh, of course it is. "I've just never seen…" I say as I bend my knees and lower to the floor to get a better look.

If a penis could hypnotize someone, I am definitely under its influence.

"Touch it," Brax says in a rough voice.

I lift my hand toward the steel and touch it with the pad of my finger. The metal is warm against my skin. "Will it hurt me?" I ask, inspecting it from every angle possible.

"No, sweetheart. It should feel better."

I peer up, my mouth agape. Better than what, I wonder, but I don't ask. I don't want to talk about Lucas and the lackluster sex life we had or the disappointing size of his dick. "Better?"

He nods as he touches my chin lightly with his

fingertips, sending sparks of electricity down my body and straight to my core. "If used right, it should."

I haven't put much thought into having a penis and if there is a right way or wrong way of using it. I thought it was in-out, in-out, in-out until it ended. "Oh," I mumble as I lean closer to the tip and lick my lips.

"You're killing me." Brax grazes my cheek with his fingers as I gawk at the length, still in a trance.

"I haven't done this often." I hate admitting that. It's so embarrassing. A woman of my age should have plenty of experience. But not me. My sex life has never been anything worth talking about with Mikayla and Sandy.

Oh my God. When they hear about his piercing, they're going to die. Wait. Do I tell them? Shit. I don't know. How can I not?

"Baby." Brax's voice pulls me out of my train of thought and back to the moment with his cock waving in my face.

"Sorry." I reach out and wrap my hands around the shaft, leaning forward to slide it between my lips.

Brax's entire body shudders as soon as my tongue touches his cock. I smile around the end, loving the way he reacts to me.

There's something so powerful about kneeling in front of him, literally causing his body to shake uncontrollably, and it has my head spinning.

"Fuck," Brax hisses.

I glance up, his cock firmly between my lips, and see his head tipped back with his mouth open.

His reaction spurs me on, making me take him deeper than I've ever taken any man's cock before. I fight the urge to gag as my lips bump against my fingers, which are still wrapped around him.

"I need more," he says, and for a moment, my stomach drops in disappointment.

Damn. I am shit at this, and I thought I was doing better than I have ever done it before.

"I need to be inside you," he growls as he leans forward, sliding his hands under my armpits.

His cock pops out of my mouth as he lifts me in the air, and I suddenly feel so empty.

"Undress," he says in a tone I don't think I've ever heard him use.

The deep, gravelly timbre of his voice makes my hands instantly go to the bottom of my V-neck sweater, ripping it off me like it's on fire.

Brax makes quick work of kicking off his pants, standing in front of me completely naked with a hunger in his eyes so intense I have an indescribable urge to throw myself at him half dressed.

"Slower," he says, taking a few steps back until his ass hits the back of a chair, and he leans on it like he's doing everything he can to soak in the moment.

I stand in front of him in my best black lace bra and a pair of jeans that are so snug I know I have a muffin top. But by the way he's looking at me, he doesn't seem to care that I'm not built like a supermodel.

"Come here." His gaze scorches my flesh as it roams around my body.

Without a single thought, my feet move, and I am in front of him a moment later. He keeps his eyes locked on mine as his fingers slide to the waistband of my jeans, making quick work of the button and zipper.

"God, you're fucking beautiful," he says to me as he peels back the thick layer of denim.

I am virtually vibrating with the need for his fingers to touch my aching body anywhere. I want the contact. No. I need the contact.

"Touch me." My voice sounds foreign and needy.

Brax's eyes flash with hunger as he lifts a single finger and brushes the soft pad across my lower stomach. I suck in a deep breath at the contact, wanting more.

My hands find his bare hips, my fingernails lightly pushing against his skin as I try to steady myself.

He curls his fingers around the top of my jeans, pushing the fabric down my hips until I drop my hands and take a step back, wanting nothing more than to be naked too. I reach behind my back, unfastening the lace bra, letting it tumble to the floor in front of my jeans.

He peers up at me, his mouth so close to the place I ache the most for him. "Step out."

I'm light-headed as I pull my feet from the legs of the jeans and try to find my footing on the floor. Brax's hand holds me up as he grips my hip and pushes himself upward until we're standing front-to-front.

And what happens next passes in a blur. He curls his hand around my neck, pulling me flush against him as his lips collide with mine. The air fills with only the sounds of our breaths, beating hearts, and mouths moving as one.

I curl my fingers around his hard length, stroking back and forth, careful to avoid his piercing. He moans at the contact, making me feel a little more powerful than I normally do.

Without skipping a beat, he snakes his arm around me before lifting me off the floor like I weigh nothing at all. My arms slide across his shoulders, and I wrap my legs around his waist to fuse myself to him. He walks backward, but I don't dare open my eyes or break the kiss.

I brace myself for impact, figuring we'll fall backward onto his bed or the couch, but that doesn't happen. He sits, positioning me on his lap. "Ride me," he murmurs against my lips.

I gasp softly. "I've never…" Lucas hated it like that and refused to even let me try, no matter how much I begged. "Are you sure?" I ask him as I pull back, looking him in the eyes.

He digs his fingertips into the soft flesh at my hips as he raises an eyebrow. "Never?"

I shake my head.

"Do you want to?"

I nod as I shift my knees, trying to find better positioning.

God, how I want to. I've always wanted to. Mikayla and Sandy always talked about how it was the best feeling and how empowering it was to be in control, and I felt completely left out.

Brax reaches over to the side table, grabbing a condom. Now, it's my turn to raise an eyebrow.

"Wishful thinking," he says as he tears open the foil, tossing the contents where the package was just lying.

I inch back, letting his cock spring free. "Are you sure this is okay?" I ask him, because Lucas had always told me how it was the worst position for a man and that was why he refused to do it. "If it's not good for you…"

Brax's eyes flash with concern as he rolls the condom over the tip of his cock and down the long, hard shaft. "Who hurt you, baby?"

"What?"

"Why would you think this isn't good? All sex is good, and this…this is going to be fucking great. I don't know who lied to you, but forget everything you've ever been told. I want you to ride me, Iris. Use me."

"Oh," I whisper, feeling a new wave of arousal even stronger than the previous one.

"You control it," he says as he moves his hands back to my hips.

I reach down between our legs as I lean forward, pressing my lips to his. I want to do this, but I can't take the eye contact while doing it.

I swipe the head of his cock through my wetness before placing it near my opening. Slowly, and I mean slowly, I ease him into me. After five gloriously torturous strokes, he's fully inside me.

His kiss becomes more demanding as I moan when he moves one of his hands to my breasts and his fingers find my nipple. Unable to sit still, needing more contact, I move my body up and down, swiveling my hips to feel the scrape of his hair against my clit.

I nearly cry out in pleasure as sensations rocket through me. I move faster, wanting more as Brax's hands roam my body, causing goose bumps to break out across my flesh.

The urge to orgasm grows stronger. My thighs burn at the unfamiliar movements, but I block that out of my mind.

"Brax," I breathe against his lips as he slides one of his hands between us and his thumb finds my clit.

I nearly jolt upward at the wicked pleasure that shoots throughout my body. It doesn't take long until he has me moving faster than I've ever moved in my entire life, bouncing up and down the length of his cock as I chase the orgasm that's bound to overtake me.

I moan, crying out his name as the pleasure crashes over me, stealing my breath. My body goes rigid as the orgasm courses through my system, but before it crests, Brax's hands find my waist again, lifting me up and pulling me down harder and rougher than anything I could ever do.

A fresh wave of pleasure overtakes me as he pounds into me before his orgasm crashes over him too.

I nearly collapse forward as all movement stops, and I gasp for air.

"Damn," I mumble, wanting to do that again and again.

CHAPTER 17
BRAX

2 WEEKS *later*

"I have an idea. You should remodel the bar," Aunt Daphne says to Lulu as she sits down at the table next to us.

Not only did Lulu handle all the wedding details, she somehow made the bar not look anything like it normally does.

She only had the last twenty-four hours to transform the old, dark space into something straight out of a modern fairy tale for my sister. We couldn't close the bar longer than that. I didn't think she could do it, but from now on, I'm never going to doubt her abilities again.

"Oh, I don't know," Lulu says, but I can see the gleam in her eyes. She's nearly salivating at the idea of getting her hands on this place.

I don't know how it looked when my grandparents

first opened it, but not a single thing has changed since I was a little kid. There is a comfort in that for me, but for customers in today's world, it is far beyond dated.

"New flooring would go a long way," I say, lifting a shoe off the tile that's been washed so many times, it no longer has a protective coating.

"Part of me loves this place," Lulu says with a sigh. "But the other part wants to tear everything out and start from scratch."

"That'll be a small fortune," Mason says, wading into the conversation.

"Not necessarily," Lulu replies. "I didn't spend much on this."

The three-piece band Lulu somehow scored on her limited budget starts to play as Wylder walks out of the back room, looking as if he's about to pass out.

The poor guy. He's been down this road before, but his first wife was a complete bitch. I don't know if I could do it again if the first time was a disaster.

Everyone in the room stands as the doors to the bar open, and Hazel and Maddy walk in, looking cute in their flowy dresses. Hazel smiles as she throws flower petals, and Maddy walks at her side, looking bored as always.

I squeeze Iris's hand as my dad and Tate fill the doorway, trying to ignore the gust of cold air that wafts through the dining room.

"She's so beautiful," Iris whispers as I stare at my sister.

She really is. She looks so much like our biological mother in their wedding photo from before we were born. I wonder if my dad's heart ached a little when he saw her today.

"She is," I whisper back as my dad and sister walk down the makeshift aisle.

Tate's eyes are pinned on Wylder, and he stares at her without moving, as if he can't do anything but watch his future solidifying before his eyes. It doesn't take long until she's in front of him with my father at her side.

Father McConnell smiles at my sister, the same priest who baptized us when we were babies. He's been a staple of the neighborhood, and although the rest of us aren't regular churchgoers, my grandparents insisted on his doing the ceremony.

"Who gives this woman to be wed?" he asks as he looks at my father.

"I do," Dad says, but his voice cracks as he places Tate's hand in Wylder's. "I love you, baby girl."

"Love you too, Daddy," she whispers to him and sniffles.

Man, neither one of them is a crier, but the emotion today is high. I know they're both thinking of Marissa, our bio mom, and how she should be here. No shade to Tilly. She's the bomb and has done everything possible to step into some big shoes. But that doesn't mean there still isn't a hole in our lives on special days like this.

Dad wipes at the corner of his eye with the backs of his knuckles as he walks over to the table to sit with his wife. Tilly gives him a sweet smile as she takes his hand before he has a chance to sit. Her gentle touch is exactly what my dad needed after losing my mom, and especially today. A lesser woman would be threatened by the emotion of missing his first wife, but not Tilly. Maybe because she lost her first husband. They're tied together in a grief that no one else would understand except the two of them.

Thankfully, the ceremony is a condensed version of the extremely long ones I've sat through way too many times to count in my almost three decades on this earth.

When Father McConnell says, "You can now kiss your bride," and Wylder sweeps Tate into his arms, kissing her a little more passionately than I'd expect in front of the family, the bar erupts into applause. I don't know if they're excited for them or happy the ceremony part is over so we can get down to the party.

Tate bends down and gives Maddy and Hazel a kiss on the cheek as the girls practically levitate with excitement. It's the first time I've seen Maddy look that happy, and it's because of my sister. She has that effect on people—well, not me because she's a pain in my ass, but on everyone else around her.

"What's your dream wedding?" Zoey asks Iris.

I don't turn my head, but I'm totally eavesdropping. Is she the type that wants the big, lavish affair? Probably. That would be my luck. I'm a simple guy, and something like Tate and Wylder just had would be plenty. I'd be fine if it were only the two of us.

Whoa.

I almost stop breathing as I realize my mind went there. Iris and I have only known each other for a month. How in the world am I already putting thought into such an important event? We haven't even said I love you yet.

Do I love her?

I do. The best parts of my days have everything to do with her. Whether it is a text, phone call, or sitting on the couch to watch a movie, everything with Iris is perfect. It frightens me sometimes too. I've never been as comfortable around someone, and it was never this easy.

"I've always dreamed of a small ceremony on the beach, even if it's only the two of us. Something simple," Iris replies, surprising the heck out of me.

"Eloping is hot," Zoey says.

Who the hell says that? My cousin, of course. The free spirit. She'd elope and probably not even tell anyone about it until after the fact, causing an uproar in the family for hiding something so big.

"You think?" Iris asks Zoey as she reaches for the champagne glass on the table.

"Totally. Shoes or no shoes?" Zoey says.

"No shoes."

My inside recoil at the thought. The only thing I hate more than walking through the snow is shoving my feet in sand. It gets everywhere and sticks to my skin far too easily.

"Sandals, at least," I add, wading into their conversation.

Zoey wrinkles her nose. "Still not over your sand issue, cousin?"

I shake my head. "Never will be."

Iris turns her dark eyes toward me with the corner of her lips turned up. "Sand issue?"

I shrug. "It gives me the creeps."

Iris chuckles. "It's nice to know you have one flaw."

"Flaw?" I ask and bark out a laugh. "It's hardly a flaw. I don't think most people like sand on their feet."

"I'd wiggle my toes in warm sand every day if I could."

My lip curls. "You could torture anything out of me like that."

"Noted," Iris says with a small laugh. "I hope I never have to use that method, but it might be worth a few laughs."

I raise an eyebrow, hoping she'd never be that mean and that I'd never give her a reason to be either. "You have to have something that gives you the icks."

"Hmm," she mutters as she lifts the champagne flute to her lips. She stares at me as she takes a tiny sip. "Those weird washcloths."

Weird washcloths? It takes me a moment, and then it dawns on me. I hate them too. "Microfiber," I whisper. "I hate those too."

"Ah. You two weirdos make the perfect pair," Zoey says as she raises her champagne glass in our direction.

"Zip it," I tell her, but I'm joking, and I know she is too. Zoey is the epitome of quirky.

Hazel comes barreling toward me out of nowhere, and before she can collide with me, I open my arms, hauling her close. "Hey, bean. What's up?"

"I'm not a bean. I'm a nut."

"Ah, yes. You're a Hazelnut," I say to her, giving her a squeeze as she squeals. I love this kid. She's a hoot. Smart as a whip and has the best sense of humor.

"Did you see me throw the flowers?" she asks as she situates herself in my lap.

"I did, and you did an excellent job."

"Thank you," she says as she beams up at me with the biggest smile.

"Have you met Iris yet?"

"Iris?" she asks as her eyes slide to my side, where Iris is seated.

"Iris, this is my niece Hazelnut, and Hazelnut, this is my girl, Iris."

"Ooooh," Hazel sings. "You're his girlfriend?"

Iris nods. "It's nice to meet you, Hazelnut."

"It's Hazel."

Iris smiles. "Hazel."

"Only he calls me Hazelnut."

"Oh," Iris says. "I'm sorry."

"Be nice, Hazel," I tell her, but I know her well enough to know there's no malice in her words.

"I mean, I like my name, but I let you call me Hazelnut sometimes, but I really like bean."

"You move around enough to be one," I say to her.

"You're really pretty," Hazel says to Iris, touching the material of her dress. "He likes you."

Iris's eyebrows rise. "You think?"

Hazel nods. "He never brings any other girls around. Just you."

"How did you get to be so smart?" I ask Hazel.

She peers up at me and, with a straight face, says, "I was born this way."

Iris covers her mouth to hide her laughter. Damn kid. She's too much at her tender age. When she gets older, she's going to be a force to be reckoned with.

Before I can say anything else, Hazel wiggles off my lap and takes off across the room to where Maddy's standing.

"She's something else," Iris says at my side.

"She's trouble in a few years," I say, watching her and Maddy giggle about something.

"She's going to break a lot of hearts," Iris adds.

"More like she's going to crush a lot of souls and pulverize a bunch of egos," I reply, turning my attention back to my date. "So, you want to elope?"

Iris's eyes go wide. "Now?"

Well, crap. I didn't mean it like that. Sometimes my mind doesn't work the way I want it to, and my mouth definitely does its own thing too. Her answer wasn't a flat-out no, which is kind of nice.

"Shit. I didn't mean now. I just meant that's your dream wedding. It's not what I thought you'd say."

"The dream has changed over time."

I wince, having forgotten about Lucas and that entire clusterfuck where he left her at the altar. I wouldn't want to stand in front of my family again with that memory burned into my brain.

"I like it. You'd pick sand over Vegas?"

She nods. "Vegas is okay, but there's nothing more beautiful than the ocean at sunset."

Lulu comes back to the table and sits down. "What are you two talking about?" she asks, being her nosy self.

"They're talking about their wedding," Zoey answers.

Lulu's mouth drops open.

"Iris was telling Zoey about her dream wedding, and I was asking questions."

"Should I start planning?" Lulu asks, ignoring the part of my sentence that said it was her dream and not about to be reality.

"You're the best, Lulu," Iris says to her. "If we ever get there, you're the first person I'll call."

Lulu touches her chest as her lip trembles. "You'd want me to do it?"

Iris nods, giving Lulu a smile. "You did an amazing job here. There's no one else I'd trust besides you."

"Maybe you should do this as a job," I tell Lulu, trying to get off the topic of Iris's wedding.

"I don't know," she says, but she doesn't finish the statement because her mother calls her from across the room. "Be back."

And with her departure, we're finally able to drop the conversation of our wedding.

"Well, aren't you two a sight," Ma says as she walks up to us with her arm looped around Dad's elbow.

"Hey, Ma." I lift myself up and kiss her cheek as she leans over to make it easier. "How you holding up, Pop?" I ask as soon as my ass is back in the seat.

He grabs two empty chairs from the table next to us and moves them around our table to sit with us. "I'm good. Good."

Tilly waves her hand in the air. "It's an emotionally difficult day for him."

"I'm sure," I say, watching his facial expressions carefully.

Dad scratches at his neatly trimmed beard. "The ceremony had a few moments that my heart hurt for Marissa missing this day, but I'm okay now. I'm too happy for your sister to let sadness become the thing I remember the most from today."

"Ma's here with us," I tell him, patting his knee. "She's watching us from above."

He gives me a sad smile. "I know, kid."

"I felt her here with us. I believe our loved ones never leave our sides, even if we can't see them," Tilly adds as she rests her head on my dad's shoulder.

"I like the thought of that," Iris says as she hooks her arm with mine and slides her hand into my palm.

Tate and Wylder move around the room, stopping to talk to various friends and family who want to congratulate them on their nuptials.

When they finally make it to our table, they look exhausted but happy.

"Congrats," I say, holding out a hand to Wylder as my dad and Tilly talk to Tate.

"Thanks, Brax." He gives my hand a firm shake before his eyes swing to Iris.

"It was a beautiful ceremony," Iris tells him.

"I couldn't have asked for anything more. I didn't need anything besides Tate and my girls."

Wylder's a big softy. He'd never admit it, but the guy is a girl dad through and through. Any hard shell he did have, Tate shattered, making sure he let go of any notion he was in charge.

"Baby brother," Tate says when she looks at me, dressed in a beautiful floor-length white gown.

I rise to my feet and kiss her cheek. "Congratulations, big sis. Another week and that dress would've given away your secret," I whisper in her ear.

"It won't be a secret much longer. We're going to announce the baby in a few days," she whispers back as Mom and Dad talk with Wylder.

If they're happy about the wedding, they're going to lose their minds over the first grandchild to be born into the family.

"Dinner's about to be served," Lulu says, staring down at her phone. "The caterer has said it's all ready to roll."

"Great. I'm starving," Tate says to her.

I'm sure she is since she's eating for two.

I was worried when she wanted to use the bar that we'd have to feed everyone too. The logistics of that would've been mind-boggling. It's hard enough when it's a family dinner, but add Wylder's side of the family and their friends, and we were bursting at the seams. At least Lulu had the good sense to find a caterer who could serve a small army on short notice.

Coordinating everything could've been a nightmare, but Lulu's organizational skills are top-notch. Any doubt I had in her has been wiped away with this event.

"Save a dance for me," Tate says in my direction before she takes Wylder's hand and heads toward the main table where their meals are being placed.

I watch my sister, seeing her smile and laugh with her new husband. Never in a million years did I think she'd find someone who would put up with her attitude, but she found the perfect man for her. And that's all anyone could ask for.

Finding your forever isn't always easy. Hell, it doesn't happen for everyone. But I have a feeling my future is next to me, and I'll do whatever it takes to keep her there.

CHAPTER 18
IRIS

"HAS EVERYTHING DIED DOWN?" Mikayla asks, catching me off guard.

"Everything?" I ask her, confused about what she means by everything.

"The Lucas thing. No sighting of anyone strange lurking around?"

I shake my head as I sip my mocktail. Brax isn't coming over tonight, and I'm not going to risk drinking and being alone. Who knows what I would do if left to my own unconscious devices. "Nope. Nothing."

Sandy leans back into the booth, twisting her martini glass between her fingertips. "Well, thank goodness for that. He's officially in your past."

"I thought he was before until he called me out of the blue."

"He's a weasel," Mikayla says, curling her top lip. "I never liked him."

"Never?"

She never said a bad word about him when we were dating. She didn't go out of her way to say good things, but she never said anything negative or that would give me pause when I accepted his proposal.

"Never." Her voice is firm as she says that word. "There was always something off about him."

"And Brax?" I ask her because she hasn't said anything bad about him either, and now I'm wondering if she's remaining quiet or if she truly likes him.

"Solid family. He's kind. Good-sized penis," she says.

I nearly cough out my drink. "Good? It's more than good."

"Okay… He's well-endowed. Better?"

"It's pretty."

Sandy snorts. "No penis is pretty."

"Decorated ones are," I say quickly.

Mikayla's eyebrows shoot up. "What? You never told us that little bit. What kind of decoration are we talking about?"

"He has a piercing."

Mikayla swats my hand. "Bad girl for not telling us that earlier."

"I didn't know you needed to know everything about his…you know."

"We don't need to know everything, but a piercing is crucial information," Mikayla says.

"It is?" I ask.

She nods. "What kind are we talking about?"

I stir my drink, wishing it were alcohol at this point because talking about Brax's penis with my friends feels like a situation where I should be thoroughly sauced. "Metal."

Mikayla rolls her eyes and groans. "Well, no shit, but what kind?"

I shrug a shoulder. "I don't have a clue about any of that."

Mikayla abandons her drink and picks up her phone, tapping away on the screen. I glance at Sandy while she does that, and Sandy gives me a quick shrug.

"What are you doing?" I ask Mikayla.

She turns the phone screen toward me, and it's littered with penises of all sizes, and each one of them has a different piercing. "Which one?"

It feels all kinds of wrong to be looking at so many, especially ones of people I don't know. But my eyes catch on one that looks like Brax's, and I point at it.

"Nice," she says as a smile pulls at her lips. "Ampallangs are sweet."

"Lemme see," Sandy says, pulling Mikayla's phone away from me. "Ooh. That's hot."

"Did you feel it?" Mikayla asks me.

"I think so."

"Did you orgasm while he fucked you?"

I glance around the bar, wondering if anyone can hear us. "Yes," I admit.

Mikayla's smile grows wider. "About damn time you found a man who can please you."

"That one's a keeper," Sandy says, handing Mikayla back her phone. "He's got a good family who seems to like you, solid job, and he's good to you. What more can a girl ask for?"

"There's more to relationships than that," I tell her.

"Right. I forgot. He gave you an orgasm. Can't forget that important nugget," Sandy adds.

"He has my nod of approval. Something Lucas never had," Mikayla says. "He better put a ring on it."

"I don't know if I'm ready for that."

"Not every man is a shithead like Lucas, baby," Mikayla says, pressing a few more buttons on her phone. "I got to run. I have a date with a hot fireman tonight, and he's waiting on me a few blocks away."

"This was your pregame?"

"Yes, Iris. That way, when I have two drinks with him, he won't know I've really had three. I don't want to seem like I have a drinking problem."

"You put thought into it. Maybe you do have a drinking problem, Mikayla," I tell her.

"I have a man problem. They're different," she explains as she leans over to kiss my cheek and then kiss Sandy's. "You two have fun. I know I will." She laughs as she strolls away from us and heads toward the door.

"You want to go? I'll walk with you," Sandy offers. "I'm over the bar scene tonight."

"Yeah, I'm ready," I tell her, fishing out two twenties from my purse and tossing them on the table because it's my turn to pay.

Sandy talks the entire walk, telling me everything about the guy she's seeing, who sounds like a complete douchebag, but she seems happy. That's all that matters. The bar is only two blocks away from my place, and Sandy lives in the next building. Although it's close, my toes go numb in my boots on the short walk. I fight through the frigid temperatures because it's better than trying to find parking near the bar.

"Well, call me if you get bored. I'm just going to binge something." Sandy gives me a kiss.

"I think I'm going right to bed. It's been a long week."

"The weather doesn't help," she says to me as I kiss her back.

"That it doesn't."

"Bye, babe," she says as she takes a step away from me.

"Bye, girly pop."

She laughs as she turns her back, heading home.

I stay on the sidewalk, waiting for her to make it to her building before I head toward the entrance of mine. A girl can never be too careful, especially when it's dark outside.

The doorman to our small building isn't in the lobby to greet me. Sometimes he disappears into the storage room to find a package or to take a quick break from the monotony of sitting by himself for hours.

I opt for the stairs instead of the elevator to get to my third-floor apartment, wanting the exercise and because I don't entirely trust the old elevators in the building either.

The Christmas wreath I haven't taken down yet is crooked on my door, and I push it a little to the side to make it right again before I unlock the door.

When I step inside, I'm blasted by the hot air against my cold, exposed flesh. I sigh, wishing I could live somewhere tropical because my body wasn't meant for the cold.

I get one arm out of my coat before I hear, "Don't scream."

In a situation like this, I'd like to think I would scream. That my voice could wake the dead. But when faced with a fight-or-flight-mode situation, my entire body locks up like I'm frozen.

Lucas steps out of the dark kitchen into the soft light of the living room from the few lamps I left on. "I needed to talk to you."

I touch my chest, trying to get my heart to calm down once it starts to beat again. "What are you doing here?" I ask in a rush as I tear off my coat and let it drop to the floor. I don't bother taking off my boots because I may need them to run. At least I still have that much sense left in my head.

"I need a place to hide out."

"And that's my problem, because?" I ask him, lifting my chin as I cock my head.

The balls on this guy. A man who shattered my heart. He wants me to do him a favor when all he's done is bring misery into my life.

"Nowhere else is safe for me."

I remember a time when I thought Lucas was my safe place and person. Boy, how I was wrong. Even now, he's more worried about his life than making sure I keep mine.

"You're not staying here."

My phone vibrates in my pocket, and I pull it out, seeing a message from Brax.

Brax: I'm off early tonight. My brother took over. I'm headed to your place for the night. Halfway there.

"Whoever it is, don't answer them," Lucas says like he's somehow the one in control.

"Fine," I tell him, because I know once Brax gets here, all hell will break loose.

All I have to do is keep Lucas talking without him laying his hands on me. He doesn't look quite like himself. His eyes are sunken in, and his clothes are disheveled. Gone is the businessman I fell in love with. It was all a façade to hide the ugly underneath.

He never physically hurt me before, but the man standing in front of me in no way resembles the person he was before.

Now, he is running for his life. And when someone's back is against the wall, anything is possible.

I need to remain calm, something I'm not always good at, and keep him far enough away from me so that I don't freeze up again.

Brax is coming. He'll fix this. He'll protect me.

"It'll only be for a few days," he says to me, pulling me back to the favor he somehow thinks I'll be willing to grant him.

"No, Lucas. You're not my problem anymore. You made sure of that a long time ago. You're on your own."

Lucas stumbles back into my favorite recliner and sits as he looks up at me with pleading eyes. When we were a couple, that look got him almost anything he asked for, but now…nope. "Do you want me to die?"

Oh. He's tugging on the heartstrings, thinking I'm the same girl he asked to marry him. She died a long time ago and doesn't care one bit about the hole Lucas dug himself into.

"Were you doing this shit when we were together?" I ask, remaining by the door.

"What shit?"

"Borrowing money from gangsters, Lucas. Don't play stupid."

He runs his hand through his hair, making the wild mane look a bit crazier. "No." He exhales and hangs his head. "Maybe."

I sigh, hating that I didn't see all the signs back then. I could've saved myself a lot of heartache if I hadn't been so blinded by my love for him.

"What the hell did you need two million dollars for?"

He lifts his head slowly, and there are tears in his eyes. Do I think they're tears of remorse? Absolutely not. He's worried about his life, but he had no problem coming here and putting mine in danger...again.

"I fucked up."

"Well, duh. But how?"

"I lost all my client's money and needed fast cash to make the problem disappear. I thought I could make it all back by shorting the market, but I was wrong."

Wrong is an understatement.

What a dumbass plan.

"How did you lose their money?" I ask to keep him talking.

"Same way I lost the two million," he whispers.

I roll my eyes. The man I once thought was so smart is really as dumb as a box of rocks. That's what my dad would say about him if he heard this stupidity.

"Give me until tomorrow at least," he continues to

beg. "I need one good night's sleep, and then I'll be gone forever. Your new boyfriend doesn't even have to know I was ever here."

He's about to get a rude awakening when Brax shows up. Hopefully traffic isn't bad or there isn't an accident on the Kennedy. "Only one night?"

Lucas nods. "Only one."

He looks so hopeful, I almost feel guilty that his excitement won't last long. But I need to keep him calm until Brax shows up. "Fine. One night and then I never want to see you again."

"Thank you," he breathes.

"The spare bed is made up. I don't want to see you until the morning."

He stands, wiping his palms against his pants. "Got it. I'll get out of your hair."

"And I want you gone before I get up," I tell him, trying to play along and make this as believable as possible.

He nods. "I'll be gone at sunrise."

"Good."

"It was nice to see you, though, Iris."

"I can't say the same, Lucas."

It feels empowering talking to him in this way. There's no softness to me. No hurt left. No tears of sadness for the ways he hurt me. He no longer means anything to me, and he can finally see that.

He gives me a sad, one-sided smile before he

leaves me standing in the living room and heads into the spare bedroom, closing the door.

I immediately text Brax.

Me: Lucas is here.

Brax: WHAT?

Me: He was in my apartment waiting for me. He wanted a place to stay. I told him he could use the spare bedroom because I was too scared to kick him out, and I knew you were on the way. He's in there now, and I'm by the door with my boots on, waiting for you.

Brax: I'm parking now. Don't go near him.

He didn't need to add the last part. I'm not about to go into the bedroom and continue having a conversation with Lucas.

The few minutes it takes Brax to park and come upstairs feel like hours. My heart leaps as I hear the ding from the elevator a few doors away.

I press my ear to the wood, listening for his footsteps, and as soon as he's close, I open it. "Hey," I whisper.

His face is nothing short of rageful, but I know it's not aimed at me. "Is he in there?"

I nod. "Back bedroom."

"Go down the hall or to the lobby. I'll deal with him," he demands in a tone I've never heard from him before.

I'm not about to argue. I want to be as far away

from Lucas as possible because I know this will turn physical, given that Lucas is fighting for his life.

"Be careful," I tell Brax.

He wraps his hand around the back of my neck, hauling me forward for a kiss. His eyes search mine for a brief second before his lips crash down on mine. "Go," he murmurs against my mouth as soon as he breaks the too-short kiss.

I hate to walk away and leave Brax alone with Lucas. I have full faith that Brax can handle him, but what if Lucas has a weapon? It never even crossed my mind because the man I was engaged to never would've carried a gun. But this version of him may very well be willing to do the unthinkable to keep himself alive.

I don't bother with the elevator, opting for the stairwell again. I haul ass down the steps to the lobby, coming to a stop when I rip the door open.

"Hey there, Ms. Iris," the doorman says as his eyes study me longer than normal. "Something wrong?"

"No, Mr. Williams. I forgot to get my mail earlier," I lie, and it slides off my tongue like warm butter.

"Gotcha," he says, finally smiling at me like he always does.

But then I realize Brax is going to haul Lucas downstairs, and Mr. Williams is going to have a lot of questions.

"Mr. Williams, do you remember Lucas?"

"Your ex?" he asks.

I nod. "He broke in to my apartment tonight, and my boyfriend is upstairs dealing with him. I don't want you to panic," I say just as he's reaching for the phone, probably about to call the police. "He's taking care of him and will remove him from the building. I just wanted you to be aware of the situation."

"Do you want me to call the cops?"

I shake my head and walk up to his desk, leaning against it because my heart is going so fast I'm scared I'm going to faint. "No. We have it handled."

"Do you need your locks changed? I can have that done for you tomorrow."

"Please," I say, hanging my head to take a few deep breaths. "He obviously still has a key because the door was locked when I got home tonight."

"It'll be done, Ms. Iris."

I smile at Mr. Williams. He's always been such a huge help, and I don't think the building would be the same without him.

The elevator doors close in the lobby, and I know exactly where they're headed. Mr. Williams and I stand in silence, staring at the spot where the doors will open and hopefully Brax will have Lucas under control.

"Come back here, Ms. Iris," Mr. Williams says, motioning in my peripheral vision for me to get behind the desk. "We don't know what's going to be behind those doors."

Shit. He's right. I assume Brax is going to have Lucas, but what if he doesn't? What if Lucas runs out and Brax is nowhere to be seen.

I hold my breath as the elevator dings in the lobby and the doors slide open. Brax has Lucas over his shoulder, and he's knocked out cold.

"I got him," Brax says as I rush toward him. "I'm taking him out of here."

"Where?" I ask.

"The less you know, the better," he replies, leaning forward to kiss my lips.

His right eye is red and there's already a bruise forming, but it looks like Lucas got the worst of it.

"Are you just going to dump him somewhere?" I push, wanting to know more.

"Something like that," he whispers.

"Let me get the door for you, sir," Mr. Williams says, rushing around his desk to grab the giant glass door to the building.

"Are you coming back?" I ask Brax before he has a chance to carry an unconscious Lucas out of the building.

"Hopefully," he says without a second look.

CHAPTER 19
BRAX

"WHERE IS HE?" Iris asks as I collapse into her bed, exhausted from the last few hours.

Nothing about the night went how I'd planned. Did I have a nice evening with my girlfriend? No. Did I get to bed at a decent hour curled up with her? Absolutely not.

"I don't know," I tell her, wishing I could make the last few hours disappear.

Iris looms over me, still dressed with her makeup on. "You don't know?"

"He's not our problem anymore."

Her eyes widen as she gazes down at me. "Did you…" Her voice falters as her eyes widen. "Did you call Malakai?"

I push myself up on my elbow as she falls back on her butt, looking completely shocked. "He broke in to your apartment. He could've hurt you or, even worse, killed you. He was becoming a thorn that would never go away. I made sure that prick has been removed from the possibility of ever hurting you again."

Her mouth hangs open as she stares at me. "I can't believe…"

"Baby, I'll do whatever it takes to keep you safe, and that includes handing over your demented ex-fiancé to a man he borrowed two million dollars from, knowing the consequences if he didn't pay him back."

"They're going to kill him," she whispers behind the palm of her hand.

"Does it matter?"

God, I sound cold. Maybe I am. I can't feel bad for a guy like Lucas. He was willing to put her life at risk in order to save his own. I can't have anything except disgust for men like him. He's a weasel and a thief.

Iris blinks a few times, gawking at me. "But…"

"Would he have let you die?" I ask her.

"I…"

"Would he have given you to Malakai to wipe his debt away?"

"I…" she says again.

"Would he have shed a single tear if you were hurt because he borrowed the money?"

This time, she doesn't open her mouth in response.

"Would he pick you over the money?"

Her head falls forward because she knows the

answers to my questions. A man like Lucas would never pick her over his own life. He was ruled by money and never by love.

"I feel so foolish," she says as she twists her hands in her lap, unable to meet my eyes. "I thought he loved me."

I reach out, taking her hand in mine. "He probably did in his own way, Iris, but not in the way you deserved."

She lifts her head, dragging her gaze to mine. "He loves money and nothing else. How could I be so stupid, Brax?"

I pull myself up to sitting, facing her on the bed. "You're not stupid, baby. You trusted someone with the most precious thing of all, and he stomped on it. Never give your heart to someone again until they prove they'll put you above themselves. Got me?"

She nods as her lip trembles. "All of this put your life in danger. Getting wrapped up with Malakai at all was a risk for you and your grandfather."

"Don't worry about us. We've dealt with men like Malakai our entire lives, and all that matters is that you are safe from here on out. Safe from Lucas and Malakai."

"Do you think Malakai killed him?"

I shake my head. "No. What good is he dead? Malakai would still be out the two mil, but I think Lucas will be paying off the debt for the rest of his life and probably get more than a few broken bones and bruises along the way."

Iris winces. "I don't know if that sounds better."

"It's his problem. Not ours or yours."

Iris slides across the bed, climbing into my lap. "I was so scared tonight."

I wrap my arms around her, holding her tight. "I can imagine. I'm sorry."

She snuggles against me, nuzzling her face into my neck. "The only thing that kept me from losing it was knowing you'd save me."

"I'd do anything to keep you safe, Iris," I whisper against her hair as I stroke her back. "Anything."

"Brax," she whispers and pulls away from me to peer up, staring me right in the eyes. "I love you."

"I love you too," I say, the words sliding off my tongue far easier than I ever imagined.

I've never uttered those words to anyone except my closest friends and family. They are too sacred to me, something not to be said lightly. Any relationship I'd had before ended when the woman professed her love and I couldn't bring myself to say it back... until now.

Iris takes my face in her warm hands, her eyes searching mine. "You do?"

I nod, pulling her closer to me. "I would move heaven and earth for you. I would choose you over me if it meant that you could experience another hour, another day. You are the most important thing in the world to me."

It's funny how fast life can change. Two months ago, I didn't even know Iris existed. Now, she is the center of my world. It happened so quickly, I'm not sure I can wrap my head around the way it all went down.

"I can't imagine my life without you now. How wild is that?"

She's thinking exactly what I am. None of it makes sense, and somehow, I understand it completely.

I fall backward, taking Iris with me. I slide my hand up her spine until my palm finds the warm skin at the back of her neck. "I hope you never have to find out what it's like," I whisper, staring up into her dark-brown eyes.

I pull her head down, wanting and needing to taste her lips and remember she's alive. She's okay. Lucas didn't hurt her before I had a chance to save her. If my brother hadn't shown up and told me to go hang out with my girl, what the hell would've happened?

I push that thought away as her lips touch mine, making the entire world disappear except for us in this moment.

My other hand finds the hem of her nightgown and slips underneath, splaying against the warm and bare skin of her ass. I growl in appreciation as my cock grows so hard and stiff, the denim of my jeans becomes painful.

I want to be in her. I need to be in her.

I push us up, breaking the kiss to pull off my T-shirt as Iris watches me, her eyes skating across my bare chest.

"God, you're so pretty," she whispers as her hungry gaze lingers.

Climbing off the bed, I start on the button of my pants, making quick work of it and the zipper. My pants are off a few seconds later, and my cock waves around in appreciation of being set free.

"I'll never get tired of seeing that," she says, her eyes homing in on my dick.

"I'll never get tired of showing it to you," I tell her before I slide back into the bed.

Her nightgown is gone a second later before she tosses it to the end of the bed, wanting me as much as I want her.

This isn't going to be a long, drawn-out lovemaking session. There is a burning need deep inside me that has been building since the moment I heard Lucas was in her apartment.

A need to know she is alive and well.

A need to know she is safe.

A need to know she is mine.

"Fuck me," Iris says against my lips as I turn us over, pressing her into the mattress with my weight.

God. There is something so dirty about hearing

those words come from her lips. Something that draws the feral part of me out of hiding.

I nestle myself between her legs, my stiff cock pressing against her opening. "I'll be gentle," I promise her, knowing she hasn't had any action besides me in the last handful of years.

"Don't," she begs, the message so clear in her eyes.

She wants rough.

She needs rough.

Any semblance of control I had slips as my lips find hers. I kiss her hard, demanding every bit of her mouth to fuse with mine, and she gives it willingly, devouring me back.

Iris lifts her legs, placing the soles of her feet against my ass, letting me know she's ready. I can't just ram my cock into her. That would be too much, too rough even if she's asking me to do it that way.

But I push my hips forward as the tip of my dick drives into her at an excruciatingly slow pace. She lets out a small moan before she whines at the speed with which I'm moving.

But she doesn't have to wait long. As soon as my cock is fully inside her, I pull back and drive into her harder and deeper than the first time.

Her fingernails bite into the skin at my sides as she holds on to me, our bodies moving as one. I've never felt something so carnal before. It's like I'm not in control of everything that is happening.

"Fuck," I groan into her mouth, wishing I could make my body move faster.

It doesn't feel like enough. It's as if I am chasing a high that I can never attain, no matter how quickly I move or how deep I go.

It doesn't take long before Iris is panting, and her body is tightening below me. But to my utter surprise, she uses all of her strength to push me over, putting herself on top.

My hands find her breasts as she starts to grind on me, taking over the entire situation. The view is out of this world as she tips her head back, hair spilling down, almost grazing my thighs. Her body comes up and thrusts down so hard, I almost become winded by the force. She is going for it, taking me harder than I was willing to take her.

"I won't last," I tell her through gritted teeth, knowing her pace is something that will push me over the edge quicker than I ever thought possible.

She ignores my words, moving faster, grinding harder against me. She is using me, and far be it for me to stop her.

I hold out for as long as I can, which isn't long compared to other times in my life. With Iris above me, using me like I'm her personal comfort toy, I can't stop what is happening.

My entire body locks up as the orgasm crashes over me, stealing my breath and making my entire body come alive. Iris follows me over the cliff, moaning out her pleasure for half the neighborhood to hear.

She collapses forward, our hearts beating at a frantic pace in time together. "I'm sorry," she says, her voice rushed and harsh. "I couldn't stop."

"Don't ever apologize for taking what you want and need, baby." I trail my fingers down her bare spine, following the path to her ass. "It's yours for the taking."

She pushes herself up on one hand and stares down at me. "Is it always supposed to be this good?"

"What?" I ask, my eyebrows pulled tight.

"Relationships."

I haven't had a ton of experience. I was always more of the casual type of guy. Anything I had that lasted longer than a few weeks happened during high school, and I wasn't banging my way through the female students.

"I don't know, but it will be with us," I promise her.

She smiles, making my heart stutter in my chest as she lies back flat against me. "I like that."

"Me too, baby. Me too," I tell her with my cock still buried inside her, although it's slowly making its way out.

I close my eyes, focusing on our hearts beating together, and drift off, dreaming of the woman I've waited for my entire life.

We are summoned before noon. My father heard about what happened last night from my grandfather. I thought the old man could keep his mouth shut for once, but of course, he had to open his big yap.

"First, are you okay?" Dad asks Iris.

Iris nods as she runs her hands down the front of her jeans as she sits in front of my dad. We're in the kitchen at my parents' house, and Tilly's gone, already at the bakery for hours.

"What happened?" he asks me, not her. "I want to hear it from you."

"Am I in trouble here? Last time I checked, I am a full-grown man." I take one of Iris's hands in mine, trying to calm her already frayed nerves.

He draws in a deep breath, the same way he used to when I exasperated him when I was a little kid and he needed a moment to compose himself. "You're not in trouble, Brax. I just need to know what happened in case there's any blowback."

"Blowback from what? We already had the blowback, and his name was Lucas."

"Malakai is dangerous."

"I know, Dad. Everyone knows that. Our business with him is done. He has Lucas, and we're out."

He stares at me with a blank face. "You think it's that easy?"

"We were never involved. Malakai only wanted

Lucas, and since he decided to break in to Iris's place, I figured I'd deliver him to Malakai directly."

"Your grandfather could've done it without you."

I shake my head. "My woman. My problem."

Dad's one eyebrow rises. "Noted."

I've never said those words or anything close to that to my father. He knows what it means. I've heard him say it multiple times in my life about Tilly.

"Your grandfather said the same thing, but he doesn't always give the whole story."

"Well, he did this time. I'm not interested in Malakai. He's not interested in me. He has everything he wants, and so do I. Lucas is out of Iris's life—and mine, by default—forever. Case closed."

Dad leans back in his chair, scratching at his beard. "Well…"

"Why don't you shave that? You're always scratching your face now."

"Your mom bought some new balm shit I keep putting on it, but I think it's giving me hives."

"Just use soap like the rest of the world," I tell him.

Dad rolls his eyes. "She thinks she's doing me a favor."

"Clearly, she's wrong."

"Don't tell her that," Dad whispers, finally using his palm to rub his skin rougher.

"Never," I mutter.

"You're done with Malakai?" he asks, somehow still not believing me.

"Forever."

He exhales loudly as his hand finally falls away from his face. "Okay."

"Do you think I'm that stupid?"

He shrugs, which shocks the shit out of me. "I'd hoped I raised you better."

"You should be talking to your father. He obviously has made some bad life choices."

"You have no idea," he tells me with a pained expression on his face. "It's surprising he's still alive."

"I'm home." Ma's voice fills the kitchen.

"She wanted to come home early to bring Iris some cupcakes," he explains when I turn toward the doorway, surprised to see her in the middle of the day.

"That's so sweet," Iris says, and I can almost hear her belly rumble from beside me.

Everyone's a sucker for Tilly's cupcakes, and if they're not, they're not human.

"I brought your favorite," Ma says to Iris as she kisses my father on the cheek where he sits across from me.

It doesn't go over my head that she brought Iris's favorite and not mine, but something about that makes my insides warm.

"You're the best, Mrs. G," Iris says, taking the box of cupcakes from Tilly's hands.

"What about me?" I ask as Iris pops open the lid to a dozen cupcakes. My eyes instantly find one of my favorites. One.

"I didn't forget you, sweetheart," Tilly says as she slips off her coat and takes the seat next to Dad.

I'm not going to get grumpy about one cupcake. She could've left me out entirely. "Thanks, Ma."

"I had more, but they sold out before I could snag them from the front. Sorry, kiddo." She smiles at me, and I know she would've brought me more if she could've.

"It's okay. I would've had to spend hours in the gym trying to work off all the sugar and butter."

"Not all women want hard planes," Tilly says to me like my body isn't a work of art.

"Do you want me a little softer?" I ask Iris as she stuffs half a cupcake between her sweet lips.

She chews the cupcake, holding up a finger while she swallows. "As long as you don't make me work out or give up cupcakes, I don't care how much time you spend in the gym or how hard your body is."

"Good," I tell her, but the cupcakes are better than the gym. I'm not one of those gymbros who lives for working out. I do it to keep in shape and because I don't get much exercise standing behind a bar all day.

"Everything sorted?" Ma asks Dad.

"Sorted," Dad replies with a soft smile.

"Good," she breathes, placing the side of her face against his shoulder. "I can stop worrying so much."

Dad and I bark out a laugh.

"That'll never happen, doll," he tells her.

Tilly's a worrier. Always has been. Always will be. But we both chalk it up to her past trauma. I know losing my mom at an early age has shaped how I act in ways I'll never fully be able to understand, no matter how much therapy I do.

"I just want all my kids to be as happy as we are," she says to my father.

I turn my gaze to Iris, who's in cupcake heaven. I don't think I've ever been this happy in my entire life. If not happy, then content. Everything around me is comfortable, which is a feeling I don't think I've ever had in such abundance before.

"I'm happy," I tell her, reaching into the box to get my lone cupcake. "Tate's happy. That leaves Mason. He can be your new project."

She groans. "He's been a project since the day he was born."

"Of course he is... He's a Gallo," Dad tells her, and no truer words have ever been spoken.

CHAPTER 20
IRIS

ONE MONTH later

I stare at the ground, nearly folded in half, with my hands on my knees and almost hyperventilating. My parents will be here in a few minutes, and the two families meeting is not only starting to feel overwhelming, but also possibly the worst idea ever.

In the dictionary, the definition of uptight has a photo of my parents, along with their names. Proper doesn't even begin to describe them. I have no idea how they're in my DNA because I'm nothing like them.

And Brax and his family are the total opposite. They are free to be who they want to be…who they are meant to be. There is never any judgment about anything. Sure, they make fun of one another every chance they get, but it is never mean or cruel, trying to get someone else to conform to their norm.

Brax's hand is light on my back, moving in soothing circles. "It'll be okay, Iris. You have to relax before you pass out."

They liked Lucas. Well, liked him before he broke my heart and ran out of a wedding they footed the bill for and still had to pay for, even after he split. He was like them. Buttoned-up, boring, and just like the perfect type of person that's portrayed on television. He was fake, and they ate that shit up too.

"This could go so wrong," I whisper before drawing air in through my nose, trying to slow my rapid breathing and the pounding of my heart.

Maybe it would be better if I passed out. All the attention would be on me and would possibly include a six-plus-hour trip to the emergency room. It's better to derail the day than for it to end in disaster.

"They're here," Brax says as a car rumbles to a stop at the edge of the street in front of the bar. "Everyone loves us, Iris. Your parents will too."

I tried to warn Brax about my parents, but he blew it off. Everyone around here loves his family, but that doesn't mean my melba toast parents will feel the same.

I lift my head, and my eyes lock with my mother's. I try to force my lips upward, but her gaze shifts to Brax, and my breath catches in my throat.

Here we go.

If I hold my breath long enough, maybe that ride to the emergency room will work. Anything to keep the two sides from meeting, right? They're oil and water, and neither should ever mix.

Mom has her hair pulled up into a tight twist and is wearing a high-collar shirt, because Lord forbid she should show even the smallest amount of cleavage. I wait for the look I've seen her give far too many people in my life.

But to my utter shock, her eyes soften as a smile spreads across her face. I blink a few times, thinking the lack of oxygen is messing with my vision.

Dad is the first one out of the car, with a hand up in greeting. "Hey, honey," he says, sounding far sweeter than I ever remember him being in my entire life. Dad isn't a mean guy, but he also isn't overly mushy. He is just as uptight as Mom but rarely shows many emotions, even in the worst of times.

"Dad," I say, but my voice rises at the end like I think his soul has been snatched up and the person inside his skin is someone else.

Dad jogs around the car, getting Mom's door. "That was an easy ride," he says as he waits for Mom to get out, and he takes her hand, helping her up onto the sidewalk.

Time seems to slow as they cross the few feet between the street and us. It feels like a movie, where they slow the film right before the big explosion to create a bigger impact and make it more jarring.

My entire body tightens as they stop in front of us. The fairy tale I've had in my head where both sides of the families get along and we live a beautiful life filled with everyone on holiday is about to go boom.

"Ma'am, it's a pleasure to meet you," Brax says to my mother, smart to greet her first over my father.

Dad is the boss, but if Mom hates you, so does my father. He doesn't have a backbone in that way. "Well, look at you," Mom says in a soft, saccharine voice. "More handsome in person than your photo."

My eyebrows furrow as she reaches for Brax to... hug him? My mom has never been a hug-strangers type of person. She barely shakes anyone's hand.

"I see where Iris gets her pretty looks," Brax says to her as he gives her a light hug back.

I almost roll my eyes, but whatever is happening here, I don't want to be the one to derail it. My parents will do that all on their own.

"Oh, you're a charmer," Mom says as her gaze moves to me. "Why didn't you tell me he's such a charmer, Iris?"

I don't answer. I don't move. I stand there wondering where my mother is. Because whatever infected my father got her too.

The two people in front of me seem so nice and are completely opposite to the two beings who raised me.

"Honey," Mom says with her arms open wide as she moves toward me.

Again, I don't move or speak. I'm too shocked to do anything except exist. I'm barely breathing as she wraps her arms around me, giving me the biggest hug I've probably ever had in my life.

"It's so good to see you. You're looking well."

"Thanks, Mom. You too," I say, unsure of what else to tell her because she's acting so weird.

"We're excited to be here." She pulls back and grabs my shoulders. "We couldn't wait to meet the man who's made you so happy."

"We're glad you came," I lie.

If I could've gone my entire life without this day, I would've.

"So, this is their bar?" Mom asks. To my surprise, there's no sneer on her face.

"Family-owned for over fifty years," Brax replies, staring at the façade of the building as my parents do. "Handed down for three generations now."

"That's impressive," Dad says as he stands next to my mother and reaches out to hold her hand.

What the hell? In all my years of life, I've never seen my parents hold hands. It was too much affection for them to show in public. Growing up with them, I find it shocking I'm not a complete prude.

"Come on in. My parents and family are all here," Brax says, holding out his arm to usher them inside.

"Everyone?" Mom asks, fiddling with the pearls she always wears around her neck. At least one thing about her hasn't changed.

Brax laughs. "My family does everything together, and that includes welcoming you to Chicago."

Mom gives me a smile. "I like him," she says.

I nearly choke on my own spit. I never ever thought I'd hear my mother utter those words.

"You do?" I ask before we make it to the door.

"Of course."

I grab her arm. "Hold on. I want to talk to you for a second." I swing my gaze to Brax. "Can you give us a minute?"

He looks at me and then to her. "Sure. Don't take long. The natives will get restless." He leans over and kisses my cheek before he takes my father inside.

"What's wrong?" Mom asks, her eyes roaming my face.

"What happened to you?"

"What do you mean?" She glances down like there might be something on her pressed white blouse.

"You're different… You both are."

Mom chuckles and reaches out to take my hand. "Your dad and I have been going to couples therapy, and then we went to this camp in Upstate New York that's for married couples looking to rekindle their romance."

My stomach turns at the thought of my parents at a sex camp. Maybe I'm wrong, but that's what it sounds like. In my mind, they had sex to have a kid, and once the deed was accomplished, they never did it again.

"While I was there, I realized how short life is and

how mine is coming to a close. I decided then and there that I was going to become a better version of myself. I want to enjoy what little time I have left, and that includes letting everyone else enjoy their time too. All that matters is happiness. Yours. Mine. Ours. Does he make you happy, Iris?"

"Who?" I ask, because I'm still processing everything she just said.

"Brax, silly."

"The happiest I've ever been."

Mom reaches out and cradles my cheek in her hand. "Honey, that is the best news. You look better than you have in years. I can see the joy in your eyes again, and I know that handsome man put it there."

And if I am honest, this is the first time I've ever seen joy in my parents' eyes too. They seem so at peace with everything, which is the opposite of the people who raised me.

"This is so weird," I whisper.

"I spent my entire life miserable, and when we went to that retreat, I realized life didn't need to be that way. I didn't have to be that way. Your father felt it too. We were both so moved by everything, we came back new people."

"Are you sure they didn't drug you or do a brain experiment?" I ask her.

She snatches me into her arms, squeezing me so tightly I practically lift off the ground. "No, baby, this is the new and better me. I'm going to spend my last however many years enjoying every single bit of life, and that includes meeting your man's family."

"Okay," I say, because what else is there to say at this point. I won't believe she is completely changed until they make it through the entire day with his family without some kind of snide remark.

"Now, can we go inside and meet everyone? It's too cold to be out here this long."

I shiver, the weather finally hitting me. I'd been too lost in thought about how body snatchers took my parents that I hadn't even felt the cold winter air against my skin. "Yes."

When we step into the bar, my dad is already deep into the dining room with Brax. They're talking to Brax's father, and my dad is laughing at something Angelo's said.

"It's all so weird," I whisper at my mother's side.

"Well, get used to it, sweetheart. This is us now. We're happy people."

"Still weird," I mutter.

"Oh my goodness. You must be Beverly," Tilly says, rushing toward my mother with her arms outstretched.

Old Beverly would've recoiled like a snake about to strike, but this version of her holds out her arms too and accepts the hug like she's been doing it her entire life.

"I'm Tilly, and we love your daughter. She's the sweetest thing."

Mom smiles at Tilly, and it's genuine, which, before today, I've never seen her pull off. "We've heard great things about Brax, and he makes our daughter happy."

"He worships her," Tilly tells her.

"I like to hear that," Mom says.

"Iris, do you mind if I take your mother to meet everyone?" Tilly asks me.

"No. Go ahead as long as it's okay with my mom."

"I'd love that," Mom says, sloughing off her winter coat and handing it to me.

I watch as my mother walks away with Tilly, both of them full of smiles as they chat and move around the room.

"What's wrong?" Brax mouths as he leaves my father's side and comes toward me.

"Those aren't my parents," I whisper.

He blinks a few times as he stares at me. "What?"

"They're too nice. Something happened to them."

"They must've changed," he replies, like that makes it normal.

"They went to a sex retreat."

"They what?"

"Mom said they went to a retreat and it changed their lives. It was a sex place."

"She said it was a sex place?"

I shake my head. "But that's what it was. Sex,

Brax." I blanch, and I am happy I have nothing in my stomach yet.

"They're adults," he says.

"They're old."

"We'll be old too someday, Iris, and I plan on still bending you over and having you as often as possible."

I swallow, my mouth suddenly dry as I gaze into his dark eyes. "I like that."

"Me too." He winks at me. "And they do too, obviously."

I groan. "I don't want to think about it."

"Well, looks like some orgasms have done them good," he says, ticking his head toward my parents, who look like they've always been here and belong around this nice family that's always so full of love.

"You said he was nice when you called them."

Brax begged for me to let him call my parents and invite them to town to meet everyone. I wasn't sure it was the right time, but then again, there would never be a good time with my parents the way I knew them to be. When he got off the phone with my father, he said it was a good talk and my dad was a cool guy. I thought he was lying to make me feel better, but now I'm not sure what to think anymore.

"He was."

My gaze travels across the bar to where my mother and father are. Tino's shaking my father's hand, but his eyes are locked on my mother. He does a funny bow and then scoops her hand up, kissing the top of it. He's a flirt, and how Betty hasn't knocked him over the head a time or two is beyond me.

"Oh boy," I mutter.

"The man never changes. He lays it on thick, thick," Brax says as I snake my arm around his back and press my body into his side.

"You're a lot like him."

He peers down at me and smiles. "You think?"

"All the good stuff, of course," I place my hand on his chest, looking out across the bar to where my parents are melting into his family easily.

Tate walks out of the kitchen with a massive tray of champagne flutes, something they never do for normal family dinners.

"What's with the champagne?"

"Special occasion," he says as he takes me by the hand and makes his way through the bar, weaving in and out of family members.

"What's the special occasion?" I ask him, following close behind so I don't walk into anyone.

"You'll see."

A moment later, we're in front of the bar and everyone in the room. Before I can ask another question, Brax drops down on one knee and is holding a box in his hand.

If I thought I was breathless outside, I'm more so now.

Brax takes my hand as the room goes quiet. "Iris,

the last few months have been the best of my life, and that's because you came into this bar and sat on the stool behind me. I never want to spend a day without you. When you're not with me, all I do is think about you. I crave you. I want you. I need you. I was yours from the moment your lips touched mine, and I want you to be mine forever." He lifts the box higher and flips open the top. "Will you do me the honor of marrying me and being mine forever?"

I cover my mouth with my hand as tears prick my eyes. The ring is stunning. I couldn't have picked out anything prettier myself. It's a simple princess cut diamond that's so big, it may look weird on my thin fingers, but I'll deal with it. Though, none of that matters. He could've made a ring out of pipe cleaners and my answer would be the same.

"Yes," I whisper and throw myself against him before he has a chance to slide the ring on my finger. "Yes."

Brax wraps his arms around me as he stumbles backward, falling on his ass. His mouth finds mine, stealing any other words I have immediately.

The room erupts around us into clapping and congratulations, but the sound is light and distant because every fiber of me is lost in the kiss.

I thought that if someone ever asked me to marry them again, I'd hesitate to give an answer after what happened with Lucas. But there is something about Brax that makes everything that came before the day we met not important or such a distant memory that it plays no part in how I react.

When we finally break our kiss, I look him straight in the eyes and shake my head. "That's why you wanted my parents to come here."

"I had to ask your dad for your hand."

"So old-fashioned."

"I'm a gentleman," he whispers against my lips.

"Lies," I say, laughing at all the times he's tossed me around and been very ungentlemanly in the bedroom. It's one of the things I like most about him.

Tate stops next to us with the tray. "Champagne?" she asks.

"Yes," I tell her, grabbing two glasses from her overfull tray.

"Congrats, sis," she says to me.

I like the sound of that. "Thanks, sis," I say back, feeling happier than I've ever felt in my life.

"So, are we eloping?" Brax asks me as I give him his glass of champagne.

"I want my toes in the sand," I tell him as I clink my glass to his.

He winces but nods. "Anything you want, you get. But I'm wearing shoes."

I lean forward, pressing my lips to his.

"Mine," he growls against my mouth, sending tingles scattering everywhere inside me.

"Yours," I breathe, and I don't think I've ever felt so loved.

EPILOGUE

BRAX

TWELVE MONTHS *later*

I stand in the doorway, arms folded, leaning against the jamb, staring at my sister and my wife. Wylder walks up behind me, filling all the open space at my side.

"Life changes fast, huh?"

"Yeah," I say to him, unable to take my eyes off them.

Tate's holding my niece Willow, and Iris has our daughter Nova in her arms. They're sharing their motherhood stories like they've been to war, and in a way, I suppose it can feel that way sometimes.

I've never been so sleep-deprived in my entire life. I'm not sure how I can even see straight most days, let alone form any thoughts. How we're supposed to keep another human alive while we're walking zombies is beyond me, but so far, we've done it.

"This stage, although exhausting, is the best."

I turn my gaze toward Wylder. "Are you crazy? I'm beyond tired."

"Yeah, but wait until they're teenagers, talking back to you, and boys are looking to get in their pants. That's worse than a little lost sleep."

My stomach twists at the thought of some grimy boy someday trying to touch my little girl. "I would murder them."

"The mouthy teenager or the boy?"

"The boy," I grumble, my fist immediately balling tightly.

"Maddy's gone on one date so far. I scared the life out of the boy. I lied to him about having done hard time and that I'd be more than willing to do it again."

I snort. "I like your style, Wylder."

He chuckles. "I would go to prison, though. I would choke the very life out of anyone who hurt any of my girls, your sister included."

"Same," I tell him.

"What are you talking about?" Tate asks, drawing our gazes their way.

"How lucky we are," Wylder says, smacking my shoulder as he strides past me to enter the living room of their house.

"Can you take her?" Tate asks, rocking on the couch like she's stuck. "I have to pee so bad. Damn bladder will never be the same."

Wylder takes Willow with ease. He's had way

more life experience with kids than me. I still get nervous sometimes with Nova. She's so tiny and breakable. No matter how many times Iris tells me she's not as fragile as she looks, I never believe her.

"Come here," Iris says to me, tipping her chin toward the empty spot on her other side. "Our girl misses you."

The babies were born four months apart, but Willow looks way older than Nova, who's just over the one-month mark. In that short amount of time, she's already grown so much that it isn't easy to remember she was ever smaller.

"There's Daddy's girl," I say, scooping Nova out of Iris's arms carefully, supporting her head in my palm. I place her on my chest, cheek against my shirt, head pushed up against my beard. She loves this. I love this. My heart hurts for the day she'll grow and no longer wants to be snuggled in my arms. The best part of my day is coming home to my girls and snuggling on the couch while the cold wind howls outside our place.

The front door opens, and Dad and Mom walk in, carrying two trays of food. "Lasagna is here," Mom calls out as Dad sets down the first tray before he takes the other from her hands. "It should be enough to freeze and have a few meals this month."

Mom's been cooking up a storm for us since we had the baby. She's been making double so Tate and

Wylder can have some too, but their food doesn't last as long since they're feeding four mouths.

"Gram is bringing the eggplant."

"Ooh," Iris whispers, rubbing her belly. "She loves me."

"She loves you and Tate the most," I tell her. "You two gave her great-grandbabies."

Iris smiles at the affirmation, but I didn't need to tell her because my grandma does every chance she gets.

"Anyone else coming?" I ask.

"Mason's covering the bar. Nino's nino'ing. And everyone else is busy. Just us and my parents," Dad says, taking Mom's coat from her before she has a chance to scurry off into the kitchen with the lasagna.

Thank God.

I love my family, but they've been spending every moment they can with us and Tate's family. The shiny new baby hasn't quite worn off for them yet, but I think we're getting close to that point...thankfully.

"Be back," Iris says, taking off toward the kitchen.

"Tilly," Hazel screeches, barreling down the stairs because she knows cupcakes are here too.

"I'll grab them out of the car," Dad says to Mom.

"Thanks," she tells him as Hazel runs into Mom's arms and squeezes her tightly.

"I've missed you," Hazel says quickly.

"Have you been a good girl? Done all your

homework?" Mom asks her as Hazel finally releases her.

"All of it. Straight A's." Hazel twists, unable to stand still when there's anything sweet involved. "Excellent behavior too. Ask Dad."

Tilly glances at Wylder, who nods. Sucker. The kid could probably burn the house down, and he'd say she's an angel. Parents may not have favorites, but no one can tell me Hazel isn't his. I'm sure there was a time when Maddy was his favorite, but I think that went out the window when puberty hit.

"Hey," Maddy says as soon as she gets to the bottom of the steps, looking every bit the disinterested teenager.

I remember those years being filled with so many hormones I wasn't sure what was up and where was down. Everything was so crazy, and my brain had to work double hard not to think about sex.

Dad walks in with two packages instead of the usual one. "I got them both."

"Perfect timing. I brought you your usual box," Mom says to Hazel, taking the top box from the stack in my dad's hands. "And for you—" she turns to Maddy "—I made sure to grab your favorite too."

Maddy's eyes widen in surprise. "Me?"

Mom nods. "A girl needs her sweets."

"If only it made her sweet too," Wylder grumbles on the other end of the couch, and somehow, I hold in the bark of laughter that was building in my throat.

"You're my favorite person," Maddy says to Mom before she turns her gaze on Wylder with a smile.

Damn. That hurt my heart, and she isn't even my kid.

"It'll take a long time," he says to me, "for her to get over what I said to that boy. But eventually, she'll understand it and will drop her attitude."

"Tate still has that attitude sometimes, so I wouldn't hold my breath," I tell him.

Who would've ever thought this would be my life? Two years ago, I didn't even have a wife on my mind, let alone a baby. But here I am now with both, and I can barely remember what my single days were like.

All I know is that I wouldn't go back for anything in the world.

I have everything I've ever wanted.

A baby.

A wife.

A life.

…and my forever.

Please turn the page to read an extended sneak peek of Need, Men of Inked Sinners #3 - Lulu Gallo's story.

SNEAK PEEK OF NEED

LULU

"Stupid car." I kick the tire, hating the potholes that never seem to go away, but only grow bigger.

I didn't even see the damn thing before my entire brain was jarred from the motion and my tire popped.

"Damn it." I bend down, staring at the rim. It's bent. This isn't going to be a simple change-the-tire job that I could do myself.

I don't really have time to deal with this today. I have a meeting with a client in two hours to go over the whole-house organization package she purchased from me yesterday. Business has really started to take off lately, especially since I began posting my work on social media. I need a car to get around the city to meet with clients and take my supplies.

I grab my phone from the passenger seat and dial the number for roadside assistance. The nice woman tells me someone will be to me within a half hour. Freaking great, but at least it won't be longer.

Me: My tire's blown.

Tate: Oh no. Want me to come get you?

The last thing I want is for Tate to come rescue me. She is a new mom and has bigger responsibilities than bailing me out for a stupid tire.

Me: No. Roadside is on the way.

Nino: What happened?

Me: Pothole.

Mason: Hate them. It's why I won't get a car.

He's lying. The boy is cheap, and he hates parting with his money for just about everything.

Amelia: At least your heater still works.

I crank it up, thankful that the car is still running since it's barely above freezing. Spring can't come soon enough.

Zoey: Lemme know where you're headed, and I'll pick you up.

Me: Can I borrow your car for the day?

Zoey: Sure thing. I'm working at the bar later.

Brax: I'll give you a ride home after work.

I love my family. Sure, they are a pain in the ass sometimes, but they are the best. Doesn't matter what kind of shit I get myself into, someone is always there to pull me out.

Me: Thanks, cousin.

Tate: Let us know when the tow is there.

Me: Will do.

I close the group chat and open my favorite app, reading through the comments on my latest post about my last job. Each video reaches a bigger audience, and although I still have a small following, it's no less exciting to see it grow.

I lose track of time on the side of the highway, trying to ignore the cars whizzing by me at such a fast speed that they could demolish my car with a mere swipe of the side.

Don't think about it, Lulu. You'll be fine. You're not going to die today.

I glance up as the rumble of a diesel engine hits my ear. The tow truck pulls in front of me and slowly backs up, stopping a few feet away.

Put a smile on your face.

Men like smiles, for some weird reason. I've been told I have a solid resting bitch face, and I need to remind myself to smile when I'm hoping someone else doesn't treat me like a douchebag. Not just any someone, but men. Women never care if I'm smiling or wearing a scowl, but any other facial expression seems to set most men on edge. Fragile egos.

I climb out of the car as the tow door opens, and a man steps out who looks big enough to block out the sun. "Ma'am," he says in the deepest, gravelly voice.

I crane my neck upward, following his torso until I can get a good look at his face. "Sir," I reply, always hating being called ma'am. I'm not old enough for that shit, but I'm more than willing to throw it back at them, hoping it rubs them the wrong way too.

The sunshine is almost blinding with the snow everywhere, and I have to shade my eyes with my hands to be able to focus on his face.

Damn. He's a stunner. He looks like he hiked down the mountain this morning after chopping a pile of wood and starting a fire by rubbing two sticks together. He's too manly to use a lighter or even flint. My mouth instantly waters at the fullness of his lips that are visible even though his beard is thick.

"Where's the issue?"

I point toward the front passenger side, unable to move from behind my door. My eyes follow his movement, soaking in his hotness.

I hate winter. It hides everything. I can't tell what his body looks like underneath his heavy coat, and I sure as hell can't see his ass because the coat's too long.

"That's going to need a tow."

I don't mutter duh, but it's on my lips. It's why I called him. "Oh no," I say, putting on the stupid-woman act, hoping it'll get this entire ordeal over sooner rather than later.

"Why don't you give me the keys and hop up in the truck to stay warm."

"Keys are in the car," I tell him. "Lemme grab my purse." I bend over, reaching across the front seat to snag my purse and phone. I glance through the windshield, and we lock eyes.

The air rushes from my lungs as I soak in his sky-blue eyes. Is there anything about this man that isn't good? Maybe he has nasty teeth, and it'll instantly ruin any fantasy I'm building with him in my mind.

"Act normal," I tell myself as I pull my upper body out of my car. "Don't embarrass yourself, Lulu."

I keep my eyes forward, not looking over at him as I start to head toward the passenger side of the tow truck. I'm doing my best to walk and not fall in the snow when I hear the man yell, "Watch out!"

Suddenly, I'm tumbling into the snow with a heavy weight on top of me, and the loudest crash I've ever heard in my life is ringing in my ears.

When I come to a stop, I'm on my back and looking up into the eyes of the hot, burly guy. "Are you okay?" he asks, his eyes searching mine.

"What happened?"

Our mouths are a few inches away, so close I can feel his warm, minty breath against my face. "A car hit yours."

I glance to the side where my car is—or, I should say, was. "Fuck," I groan, slamming my head back into the snow and squeezing my eyes shut.

If my day was bad before, it just got worse.

"Are you hurt?" the burly tow truck driver asks me again.

"I don't think so." But that doesn't mean

tomorrow I won't feel the tumble deep down in my muscles.

"Fuck. That was close."

Then it hits me. I was standing right where the car must've sideswiped mine, missing his tow truck but sending my car off into the woods on the side of the highway.

"You saved me," I breathe, my fingers touching his jeans somewhere near his ass.

"I couldn't let you die."

"You could've," I argue.

This handsome man stares down at me and, with a straight face, says, "Darlin', what kind of man would I be if I let you die right in front of my eyes if I could save your life?"

"One who has an overwhelming sense of self-preservation," I tell him.

Would I have done the same? I'm a good person, but I don't know if I could literally jump toward a moving car to save a stranger, even a hot one.

He smirks at my statement as he pushes himself off me and then holds out a hand to me.

I don't hesitate in taking his hand and being pulled up from the ground like I weigh nothing.

God, I love strong men. Smart is a bonus, but strong…that gets my motor running. Maybe that will change as I get older, but for right now, it is high up there on the list of important qualities I want in a man. Is it stupid? Probably, but I don't give a crap.

When my eyes move to where my car used to be, I suck in a breath as the realization crashes over me. A minute earlier and I would've been bending over, half inside, half outside to grab my purse. A few minutes before that and I would've been completely inside, waiting for the lumberjack tow truck driver to get here.

"Don't worry," the guy says at my side. "I have a dashcam. We'll find out who that asshole was."

I hadn't even realized the person never stopped after demolishing my car like he meant to do it. "Damn," I mutter, shaking my head. "Why would they leave?"

"A bunch of reasons. Maybe they were drunk or had an outstanding warrant."

"Asshole," I whisper and turn my gaze toward Mr. Burly. "Not you. Them." I fling my arm out toward the pieces of my car that stayed where the entire thing used to be.

He reaches into his pocket, fishing out his phone. "That they are, darlin'. I'll call this in."

"Call it in?" I ask, totally missing that he called me darlin'. In any other time, those words would've made my belly flutter, but right now, I was knee-deep in shock.

"The police."

I nod as he lifts the phone to his ear. "Right," I mutter, and I am happy at least one of us is thinking clearly.

I turn my body, staring out across the highway, and watch the cars move past in a blur. I've never been that close to dying before. If he hadn't tackled me, I wouldn't be breathing right now. It all happened in the blink of an eye, and that is the scariest part of it. One minute you're here, and the next...you're not.

"They're on the way."

"Thanks," I say, my voice soft compared to the buzz of the traffic.

The man touches my back so gently, I almost don't feel it. "Why don't you wait in the truck. It's not safe to stand here."

I can't argue with him. His point was proven a few minutes ago. "Okay," I say, sounding more like a zombie than myself.

My feet move on their own, trusting this man with every fiber of my being. He guides me toward the passenger door of his giant tow truck, which looks more like a tank compared to my cute little sports car.

"Up you go," he says after opening the door for me and moving his hand from my back to my arm. "You'll be safer in here."

"Yeah," I whisper, grabbing the bar inside the truck to haul myself up. I'm not a short girl, but this truck makes me feel dainty and little.

As soon as I'm situated, staring straight ahead, he closes the door and walks around the truck, talking to himself.

As much as this is a pain for me, I'm sure he didn't

have this on his bingo card today. What was supposed to be a simple job has now made him into a witness to a crime.

"I called my partner to tow your car out of the woods," he says as he settles into the seat next me. "His truck is built better for going off-road."

His partner. I should've known he was too good looking to be straight. Damn it.

"Thanks," I say again, but I don't think I can say it enough. There's so much to thank him for, specifically me still being alive.

"You wet?" he asks.

I snap my head to the side, and my eyes widen. "What?"

"Are you wet?" he asks again.

I blink a few times in even more shock than I was when I almost died. "Excuse me?" I finally say.

"From the snow," he explains, looking at me like I have three eyes.

"Oh," I whisper. Of course my mind went into the gutter. It's hard for it not to with the mountain man next to me. I just need to get through this day without making a complete idiot of myself.

Preorder your copy of Need, coming Summer 2025. ***Click here to reserve your copy now*** or visit ***menofinked.com/need***

Lulu Gallo's story is coming next…
visit *menofinked.com/need* to get your copy from
your favorite eBook retailers or order direct at
chelleblissromance.com

**Want to be the first to hear about the next
Men of Inked book or everything Chelle
Bliss?** Join my newsletter by visiting *menofinked.
com/inked-news*

BECOME A MEMBER OF THE FAMILY...

Want a place to talk romance books, meet other bookworms, and all things Men of Inked? Join Chelle Bliss Books on Facebook to get sneak peeks, exclusive news, and special giveaways.

Want to be the first to hear about the next Men of Inked book or everything Chelle Bliss? Join my newsletter by visiting _menofinked.com/inked-news_ or scan the QR code below.

NEED MORE MEN OF INKED CHICAGO?

THE COMPLETE DIGITAL EBOOK COLLECTION

Have you read the Men of Inked Southside series?
Visit ***menofinked.com/southside*** to learn more
and be prepared for the Men of Inked Sinners, the
next generation of the Southside.

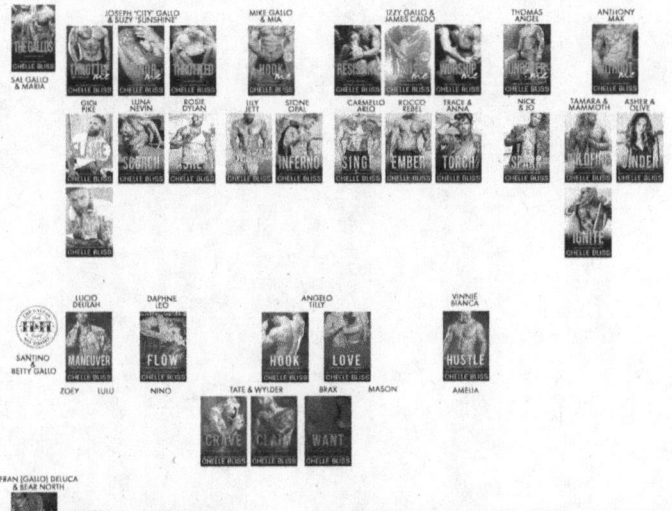

MEN OF INKED
FAMILY TREE

MENOFINKED.COM/BOOKS

Check out a bigger version at **_menofinked.com/ gallo-family-tree_** or view the series reading order at **_menofinked.com/gallo-saga_**

ABOUT THE AUTHOR

I'm a full-time writer, time-waster extraordinaire, social media addict, coffee fiend, and ex-history teacher. *To learn more about my books, please visit menofinked.com.*

Want to stay up-to-date on the newest
Men of Inked release and more?
Join my newsletter at *menofinked.com/news*

Join over 10,000 readers on Facebook in Chelle Bliss Books private reader group and talk books and all things reading. Come be part of the family!

See the Gallo Family Tree

Where to Follow Me:

facebook.com/authorchellebliss1

instagram.com/authorchellebliss

bookbub.com/authors/chelle-bliss

goodreads.com/chellebliss

tiktok.com/@chelleblissauthor

amazon.com/author/chellebliss

pinterest.com/chellebliss10